YOURS FOREVER

SHERELLE GREEN

Cover Design: Sherelle Green

Editor: LCS Literary

Manufactured and Printed in the United States of America

Dedication

To my literary sisters, Angela Seals, Elle Wright, and Sheryl Lister. I knew the moment we all sat down for dinner the first time, it was the beginning of something beautiful. I loved working with you ladies on the Once Upon a Bridesmaid series! XOXO ~Sherelle~

To all my readers who constantly support my work, thank you for giving me a reason to write beautiful love stories. I appreciate you more than you realize. Much love! (((hugs)))

THE PACT

There are two things in life that a woman always needs to have in her possession: her sanity and her punani. Grandma Pearl's words echoed in Mackenzie Cannon's mind as she fidgeted in her cushioned wicker chair and ignored the conversation taking place between her best friends.

Grandma Pearl had always been one of Mac's favorite people. Not only had she been a classy woman with her large church hats and beautiful thick figure, but she'd also been the one to teach Mac the art of talking dirty without it sounding dirty.

Granted, there were times that Mac would rather say *pussy* instead of *punani*, but she kept it as classy as she could.

"I bet he tastes as good as he looks," Mac said aloud, taking in the delicious sight of the best man in a tux. "Can someone please get me a glass of water?"

When he turned to look her way, she didn't even try to hide her thorough perusal of his body. Now that one of her best friends was married and dancing with her new husband on the dance floor, Mac could loosen her bridesmaid dress and focus on the tall cup of coffee who'd held her attention all weekend long.

"Seriously, Mac! Are you even listening to what I'm saying?"

Mac turned to face her best friend since childhood, Quinn Jacobs. They may be polar opposites, but Mac had a soft spot for Q. Despite their differences, they were extremely close. "I heard you, Q. I agree, Ava and Owen look happy. But in case you didn't notice, I'm trying my best focus on something a little more interesting than the newlyweds."

Mac, Quinn, Raven Emerson, and Ryleigh Fields had grown up in the small town of Rosewood Heights, South Carolina and had been friends since they were little girls. Although they each decided to pursue careers in other states, the women had returned to their hometown to celebrate the union of the fifth member of their pack—and the only friend still residing in Rosewood—Ava Prescott, to her husband, Owen Sullivan. The beautiful wedding had taken place in Rosewood Estates, a staple in the small lake town and perfect for a woman who valued tradition and community like Ava did.

"Why must you be so rude?" Raven asked, shaking her head. "You know how Q gets when she's talking about romance."

"Ha!" Mac said with a laugh. "Anyone within a thirty-mile radius can hear her squeal when she starts talking about love and shit."

"Girl, you can say that again," Ryleigh said, giving Mac a high-five. It was normal for Ryleigh and Mac to agree. Both were headstrong and loved cozying up to a good-looking man every once and a while. At their high school dances, they'd often place bets on who could get the most numbers. Typically, they both took turns winning.

Quinn cleared her throat. "If everyone's done making fun of me, can we please continue the discussion?"

Mac turned her body in her chair so that she could face each of the women just as the waiter approached to take their drink order.

"I'll have another mojito," Mac said as she polished off her third glass in preparation for her fourth. When it came to getting through weddings, Mac had a firm drinking rule... More booze equaled more fun.

Conversation flowed between the friends as if it hadn't been a while since they'd last seen each other. Living in different states meant a lot of emails, calls, and text messages passed between them. Despite the different area codes, they made an effort to have a group conference call at least once a month to stay in touch.

The young waiter returned with their drinks and shot her what she assumed was his killer smile. Mac barely paid the youngin' any mind.

"I think we should toast," Quinn said, lifting her margarita high. "Here's to us all finding that special someone and saying 'I do' by this time next year."

Raven froze, her glass in mid-air. "Are you *crazy*?"

"Oh hell no," Ryleigh said at the same time, almost spilling her drink when she placed her glass on the table.

Mac was shaking her head in disagreement before Quinn even got out the last word. "The only thing I'm saying 'I do' to is one night with that tall, mouth-watering best man standing over there." She glanced over her shoulder in his direction.

Quinn placed her glass down and perked up in her chair. "Oh, come on you guys! We're twenty-nine years old! I don't want to be pushing a stroller when I'm fifty."

"If Janet Jackson can do it, so can we," Mac said with a smile.

"I'm being serious." Quinn scooted forward in her chair. "Think about it. Just about everybody we know has gotten married in the last three years, yet we're all still single. Wouldn't it be nice to have a warm, hard body to snuggle up to every night? To not have to worry about those awkward bar or club meetings? I mean, how hard could it be?" She lifted her glass again. "Come on! We can do this. Right here. Right now. Let's make a pact. Better yet, let's make this a best friend challenge."

Mac winced. *Damn, Q just said the magic words.* They were

known to place a wager on anything and Mac *hated* to lose. Mac watched Raven slowly lift her glass to Quinn's. A quick glance at Ryleigh proved that she shared the same sentiment as Mac, but she slowly began to lift her glass as well.

"Oh shit," Mac huffed. "Are you seriously trying to make us all agree to be married before this time next year?"

Quinn smirked. "I thought the *Queen of Friends with Benefits* wasn't afraid of anything."

Mac rolled her eyes at the not-so-endearing nickname her friends had given her back when they were in high school. "I'm not afraid of anything."

"Then raise your glass, girlfriend," Quinn teased.

Mac hesitantly bit her bottom lip before finally raising her glass.

"To finding that special someone and saying 'I do' by this time next year," Quinn repeated when all four glasses were raised.

Mac felt like she was on auto-pilot as they clinked glasses before taking a sip of their drinks. *Screw it,* she thought as she downed her entire drink after a few more seconds. There weren't too many things that left Mac speechless, but agreeing to this pact was one for the books. *I definitely need a distraction now,* she thought as her eyes drifted back to the best man.

Mac stood from her chair. "Well, ladies, as fun as this is, I'll have to catch you in the morning for breakfast."

Quinn shook her head. "You won't find your husband by getting in the best man's pants."

Mac smoothed out her bridesmaid dress. "Sweetie, I'm sure my future husband, whomever he may be, will appreciate my sex drive. In the meantime, there are other men who will appreciate it just as much."

Was Mac ashamed that she enjoyed sex so much? Absolutely not. Would Mac ever apologize for having a frivolous fling? No way! She knew who she was and she didn't have to explain herself to anybody.

Quinn shook her head. "It's not always about sex, Mac."

"And marriage isn't always about love and romance." With a wink, Mac made her way across the room, leaving her friends to discuss how shocked they were that she'd agreed to the pact. They were probably assuming she would back out, but there was no way Mac was backing down from a best friend challenge. No way at all.

* * *

"BEWARE, my brother. You may have been tempted before, but temptation never looked like that."

Alexander Carter followed his brother's gaze, only to find the sexy bridesmaid that he'd been avoiding all weekend walking toward them. *Damn.* It was almost like she'd been plucked from every fantasy he'd ever had of the opposite sex. Her thick honey-brown curls were pulled to the side, cascading over her shoulders. Alex had always had a thing for big, natural curls and hers were no exception. His fingers itched to run through her hair.

If that wasn't enough to send his libido into overdrive, the woman had enough curves to keep a man occupied for decades. While some men always went after the skinny-model type, Alex preferred a woman with a little more meat on her bones. *And damned if she isn't stacked in all the right places.*

He cleared his throat before leaning against the bar and looking back at his younger brother, Shane. "Yeah, I'm in trouble."

"I told you, big bruh, you were in trouble the minute we went to Ava and Owen's luncheon a couple of days ago. When Owen asked us to be in the wedding last year, he warned you that Ava had some fine-ass friends."

"Yeah, but I didn't think he meant any of them were my type."

Shane laughed. "You know Owen has always been into talking in riddles and shit. He was trying to warn you without saying those exact words."

Alex shook his head. "I've been celibate for two years and haven't given into temptation. There's no way I'm giving in now."

Shane's voice lowered. "Listen, I know the face of a woman on a mission, so you have to ask yourself one question. Can you handle denying yourself a night with a sexy siren like her?"

"Yes, I can."

Shane could barely conceal his grin. "Then good luck, my brother." He glanced over Alex's shoulder. "You're gonna need it."

Shane had only been gone two seconds when she approached. "Hello, mind if I join you?"

Alex turned to face the stunning brown beauty he'd just been speaking about. *Tell her no. Send her on her way. You may have had the strength to avoid women before, but not a woman like her.*

"Sure, please do." Her thigh grazed his as she leaned next to him against the bar. Alex briefly shut his eyes. *Wrong move, my dude.*

"So, what is Alexander Carter's drink of choice?"

He took a sip of his once-forgotten drink. "Cognac on the rocks."

She squinted her eyes. "Smooth, strong, dark. At first it appears simple, but then you take one sip and experience the added element of charm and power." She looked him up and down. "I can see why you like it. It suits you."

Alex grinned slyly. "And what does Miss Mackenzie Cannon drink?"

"Today, mojitos were my drink of choice. But, usually, I'm a White Russian kind of woman."

Alex leaned slightly forward. "A White Russian… Sweet, yet robust. Creamy. The type of drink that sneaks up on you." He observed her a little closer. "And the coffee gives the drink a hint of the unexpected and plays with your taste buds."

When her eyes briefly danced with amusement, Alex noticed they were the color of sweet honey. He licked his lips and her eyes followed the movement.

"Very intuitive, Mr. Carter," Mac said as she stepped a little closer. "I'm not the type of woman to beat around the bush, so I must warn you that I came over here to try and seduce you."

Alex swallowed. "Well, I must say that you're doing a damn good job."

"Oh, I don't know about that, Mr. Carter." She pushed a few of her curls over her shoulder and placed one hand on her hip. "Although I came over here to do the seducing, you're seducing me in ways that you probably don't even realize."

Man, she needs to stop calling me Mr. Carter. Her voice was sultry and as smooth as velvet. Addressing him so formally was only making his pants tighter in the crotch area.

"Want to take a walk?" Mac asked.

If you leave the confides of this reception, you may not be able to control yourself. "Sure," he responded, ignoring the warning.

It was a beautiful September day in Rosewood Heights and Alex found the laid-back lake town extremely relaxing for a city boy like himself.

"I never thought I'd say this, but I miss this small town." Alex glanced at Mac just as she waved to a store owner across the street.

"I can understand why you miss it. I moved around so much as a kid that I don't really have roots anywhere. At least I didn't until I became an adult and settled down on the east coast."

"I know the feeling," Mac said with a laugh. "My family moved around a lot when I was younger, but for some reason, we always came back to Rosewood. And every time we returned, my girlfriends welcomed me back with open arms."

Alex smiled. He hadn't known Mac for more than forty-eight hours, but he'd pegged her as the type that didn't open up easily. The fact that she'd even told him that much surprised him.

They fell into easy conversation with an underline of flirtation in every word they said to one another. As much as Alex missed having sex, he missed the act of flirting even more. In his experience, flirting with a woman meant it would lead to other things. Things of the sexual nature. Things that wouldn't end well for a guy who'd made a vow of celibacy.

"I've done a lot of traveling, but this is still one of my favorite spots," Mac said as they approached a small garden with locks all along the fence. "We call this Love's Last Garden. It's been said that Rosewood Heights is the place where people come to relax and find love. Most of it is a myth, but this was the last garden that was built in the town and many townsfolk fell in love in this very place. Once you find love, you place a lock on the fence."

Alex looked around at the lush greenery and locks positioned about the fence. He couldn't quite place his finger on it, but he felt even more connected with Mac being in this garden. When he turned back to Mac, his eyes met hers. Watching him. Observing him. She bit her lip again in the same way he'd seen her do all day before her eyes dropped to his lips. *What is it with this woman?* He barely knew her, yet something about her drew him in. And without dwelling on his next move, he took two short strides toward her and pulled her to him.

He gave her a few seconds to protest, but when she looked up at him expectantly, he brought his lips down to hers. Alex had meant for it to be a simple kiss, but he should have known that Mac would awaken a desire deep within him, especially after the tension between them all weekend. She slowly opened her mouth and he took the invitation to add his tongue to the foreplay.

Kissing Mac wasn't what he'd expected. It was so much more. He may be celibate, but he'd had his fair share of kisses. With Mac, she kissed with her entire body, nipping and suckling in a way that was mentally breaking down the walls he usually had up. When her moan drifted to his ears, Alex pulled her even closer, tilting her head for better access. His hands eventually found their way to her ass, cupping her through the material of her dress. Although the sun had set, they kissed in a way that made Alex forget that they were standing in a public garden.

At her next moan, Alex stepped back. *Man, you need to get a grip.* Even with the space between them, he could still feel her heat. If she kissed like that, he could only imagine how she'd be in bed.

They stood there for a couple of minutes, neither saying anything as they took in their fill of one another. Being the CEO of an environmental engineer firm, Alex knew a thing or two about self-control to reach the ultimate goal. He was one of the most controlled people he knew. However, as he got lost in Mac's honey gaze, he couldn't remember the reasons why he'd decided to be celibate in the first place. *Surely there were a list of reasons, right?*

Mac stepped back to him and ran her fingers over his loosened navy blue tie. "Your room or mine?"

This was it. This was the situation he'd been trying to avoid since he'd laid eyes on Mackenzie Carter. The old Alex wouldn't have hesitated to drag Mac to his hotel room and explore her delicious body. However, the new and improved Alex didn't think it was such a good idea. His right and wrong consciousness battled with one another, each arguing their point of view, trying to convince him to take their side. *This should be an easy decision. Say no, remain celibate, and send Mac on her merry way.*

"What will it be, Mr. Carter?" She brought her plump lips to his ear. "Do you want to share a night of unrestrained bliss with yours truly?" She tugged his earlobe between her teeth before soothing the bite with a kiss.

What. The. Fuck. If there was a book on seduction, Mac must have invented it. When she boldly ran her hips over his midsection, he lost all train of thought. His eyes landed on hers and held her gaze.

"Mine," he said in a firm voice. "It's time that I show you what calling me 'Mr. Carter' does to me."

He didn't even give her a chance to respond as he tugged her through the garden and in the direction of Rosewood Inn.

* * *

"No, no, no, no, no," Mac chanted in her mind for the hundredth time in the past hour. It was 2 a.m. and the only thing on her mind was getting the hell out of Alex's hotel room before the sun rose and he woke up.

She slipped out from underneath the covers in pure stealth mode and tiptoed across the room. Even though Mac was no virgin to one-night stands, what she'd experienced with Alex had shook her to the core.

Not only had he been amazing in bed, which she'd predicted the minute she laid eyes on him, but they'd also had great conversation. She wasn't even sure who'd started it, but she knew it had to be him since she sure as hell never had deep conversations with men she never planned on seeing again.

Finding her dress, she squeezed the material up her naked body and zipped the back as high as she could, before running her fingers through her disheveled hair. The only light in the room was from the foyer by the door, but luckily, it was enough light for her to find her shoes and purse.

She glanced around the room, satisfied that she wasn't leaving anything behind. Just as her hand gripped the handle of the door, she realized she'd forgotten one very important piece of clothing.

Fuck it, she thought as she opened the door. At the sound of Grandma Pearl's words echoing in her mind, she hesitated. *If a woman is grown enough to take off her panties for a man, then she's grown enough to remember to put them back on before she takes her walk of shame.* In Mac's mind, she wasn't taking the walk of shame, but Grandma Pearl was right. She should get her panties before she left.

She lightly closed the cracked door and tiptoed back into the bedroom, flipping over tossed pillows and sheets for her panties. *There you are,* she thought when she spotted the lace delicate flung over one of the empty wine glasses.

She took them off the wine glass and bent down to put them on.

"I wouldn't do that if I were you." The deep, gruff voice chilled her bones and caused her to yelp in surprise.

"Shit, Alex. Way to give me a heart attack."

"I'm sorry," he said as he stood. Mac's mouth watered. *Does he remember that he's naked?* His smirk proved that he did, but he didn't seem to care one bit. She supposed he shouldn't after the sex they'd just had.

"Where are you going?" he asked.

"Um, I was going back to my room."

Alex glanced down at his watch which was currently the *only* thing he was wearing. "It's only a little after two."

"I know. I figured I'd get some more sleep before I have to meet my friends for breakfast."

Alex squinted his eyes before he took two strides in her direction. Mac couldn't help but to stare at his dick that was currently protruding upright, ready for round two. *So delicious,* she thought as she licked her lips. *Wait, not delicious. Dangerous. You can't handle round two with Alex.*

The entire weekend, Alex had been avoiding her, and after learning a little more about him through Owen, she'd understood that he didn't date much and was all about work. Mac knew his type, which usually worked well with her personality. The career-focused businessman often didn't have time for anything serious and was fine with a frivolous affair. Which meant, Alex was right up her alley.

There was just one major problem. The moment she'd felt Alex buried deep inside her, she knew she'd made one grave mistake. She'd underestimated the power of a big dick that happened to be attached to a sexy man with an intelligent mind, who just so happened to be caring and giving in the bedroom. In other words, instead of being exactly what she needed, he turned out to be everything she'd avoided her entire life.

"One night of unrestrained bliss," he said.

Mac blinked her eyes from their *Why in the World is His Penis So Beautiful* state. "What did you say?"

Alex stepped closer to her, his shaft poking her in the belly with such force, she was shocked she didn't get impregnated on the spot. "I just repeated the words to you that you had told me before we came to my hotel room. You said one night, and judging by how dark it is outside, it's still nighttime."

"It's technically the morning," she said quickly. "So I should go."

Alex leaned down and placed a tender kiss on her neck before moving to the back of her ear. "I'm not ready to let you go yet." He pulled her to him, his hands unzipping her back zipper as he continued to run his lips across her body. "If one night is all I get with a woman as amazing as you are, then I'm making the most of every hour. Every minute. *Every* second."

Before she could let out the breath she'd been holding, her bridesmaid dress fell into a puddle around her feet, quickly joined by her forgotten panties and purse. His words were like lava and lit a volcano inside her that was ready to erupt despite the fact that he wasn't even using tongue with his kisses.

You know you want to go another round.

Apparently, Alex sensed her internal battle because his eyes briefly softened before he turned her around so that she was facing the wall.

"Spread your legs," he whispered into her ear. The combination of his warm breath on her ear and his deep voice caused her to shiver. Despite her hesitation, she did as she was told.

His muscular arm reached around her body and fondled with her already wet folds. "Do you remember when I warned you that you'd see what happens when you call me Mr. Carter?" He brought the fingers that had been playing with her folds to his lips and sucked hard.

"Yeah," she said breathlessly. "I remember."

"Good." Taking his other hand, he cupped one of her breasts, teasing the nipple between two of his fingers, causing Mac to drop her head back on his shoulder. "I want to tell you a story," he said.

A story? She opened her mouth to ask why now was a good time for a story, but her words died on her lips when he slipped and curved two fingers inside her. Mac had never been much for fingering, but the way that Alex was moving his fingers in and out of her felt amazing.

"Lift your legs up," he said. She lifted her head and noticed two of the small tables that were previously near the bed were now on either side of her. *When the hell did he put these here?* He hadn't stopped touching her since he'd caught her trying to sneak out, so she assumed he'd set these up before they'd fallen asleep. *Unless he'd never fallen asleep.*

"I didn't."

She looked at him over her shoulder. "You didn't what?"

"I didn't fall asleep," he said.

Her heartbeat quickened. "I never asked."

"You didn't have to. I sensed that beautiful brain of yours trying to figure out how I managed to get the tables over here. In answer to your question, I never went to sleep, but when you tried to sneak out, I closed my eyes so that you wouldn't feel uncomfortable. Then, when you came back into the room, I took it as a sign."

"A sign for what?" His hands continued moving in and out of her core, making it more difficult to concentrate on what he was saying.

"More like a reminder that I wasn't anywhere near done exploring your body, and if tonight was all we had, I was damn sure gonna to make the most of it."

He twisted her around to face him and helped her stand with one foot on each table, plucking a breast into his hot mouth as he did.

"Which brings me to my story," he said after he'd paid the same amount of attention to her other breast. "There once was a wedding in a small town, and at this wedding, there was a best man who had his eye on a gorgeous bridesmaid."

He dragged his tongue across her collarbone and shoulders. "All weekend, the bridesmaid was tempting the best man, and although he didn't mind, he knew that the minute he kissed those beautiful, desirable lips, he couldn't be held responsible for the amount of pleasure he bestowed upon her." Mac shivered when he firmly gripped her ass, steadying her when she shifted on the tables.

"When the best man finally tasted those sweet lips, he knew he'd been right. Suddenly, it wasn't about the fact that they were strangers. Nor was it about the fact that they probably shouldn't start anything that they couldn't or *shouldn't* finish. Instead, the only thing that mattered was how many orgasms he could give her before she disappeared into the night."

Mac's mind was racing with thoughts of if she should get off the tables, grab her clothes, and hightail her naked ass out of there, or wait and see what happened next.

When he dropped to the floor and enclosed his mouth around her clit as his fingers continued to move inside of her, she stopped thinking entirely. Within seconds, she exploded in a powerful orgasm, her knees locking in their position as she thanked her lucky stars that Alex was beneath her to help steady her movements.

He lifted her with ease and placed her on the nearby desk. The position wasn't extremely comfortable since she was lying on notepads, pens, and partially on the phone in the room, but seconds later, she didn't care when his mouth found her center again.

"What makes you think I can take another one so soon," she said.

"Because you can," he said between suckling her clit. "The

female anatomy is a beautiful thing." He didn't ease up the onslaught of his tongue and before long, she was exploding in another orgasm and gripping the desk so hard, her nails chipped the mahogany wood.

Alex lifted her again, placing her on the bed this time. *Holy crap.* Mac's mind wasn't just in the stars, it was in an entirely different universe. She was just coming down from her high when she noticed he'd put on protection and helped her get on all fours.

"If you want me to stop, just say the word," he said as he rubbed her ass. The circular motion of his thumbs as they caressed her was calming and arousing at the same time.

"I'm good," she said, accepting the inevitable. "Don't stop."

She couldn't see the sly smile on his face, but she felt it in his next words. "I was hoping you'd say that." She didn't predict where his tongue that was gliding along her butt was going until he was close to her DO NOT ENTER zone.

"Oh my God," she said, when his tongue dove into a place that made her want to weep in surprising pleasure. "Pleasure this good feels wrong on so many levels."

"I don't know," he said as he took another thorough lick of her ass before biting a butt cheek. "Feels like this is exactly where I'm supposed to be."

That's the problem, she thought as she writhed under his mouth. After a few more licks and bites, his fingers ran up and down her vaginal folds. Without warning, he entered her in one *long* stroke. The move made her cry out in pleasure, her voice bouncing off the headboard.

Even in the midst of passion, Mac couldn't help but reflect on everything that had happened tonight. *Alex is a sex god.* If there was anything that any man remembered about Mac, it was that she in no way, shape or form ever called a man a sex god. To Mac, women were the real champs because they gave their partners pleasure while ignoring their own wants and needs just to make the other person happy. Mac definitely didn't practice that rule, but she knew a lot of women who did. *Those women clearly never met a man like Alexander Carter.* Come to think of it, neither had she.

"The first time we did this, it was fast and quick," he said as he pulled out of her with slow precision. "This time, we're going slowly so I can feel every vaginal muscle you have clench around me. So get comfortable."

Get comfortable? Is he for real? There was no part of this experience that was comfortable for Mac. Sex with casual partners was comfortable. One night stands were comfortable. Quickies in which both parties left satisfied was comfortable. But this? This slow, deliberate sexual build-up and multiple orgasms with the sole purpose of driving her out of her damn mind was definitely *not* comfortable. Yet even knowing that fact, Mac still couldn't wait to see what the rest of the night had in store.

CHAPTER 1

wo Months Later

"If you want to keep all your fingers, I suggest that you remove your nasty-ass hand from my thigh." Mac lifted her fork for good measure.

"Dang, sista, you ain't that fly." The sleazy guy raised his hands in the air in defeat, and walked away.

"Mac!" Mac turned at the sound of her younger sister, McKenna's, voice.

"What?"

"Why must you be so rude?"

Mac's eyes widened. "Me? How was I rude? He was the one who placed his hand on my thigh without permission."

"Sis, you're in a bar and it's barely 10 a.m. What type of men do you think frequent bars in the morning?"

"I heard that," the sleazy guy said.

"Sorry, Frank. You know you're my favorite customer." Frank smiled before returning his attention back to his drink.

"Why do you always manage to offend my regular customers when you visit my bar?"

Mac shrugged. "It's not my fault that most of your regulars don't like me."

"I wonder why," McKenna said, raising an eyebrow. "Are you going to tell me why you're here so early?"

"For your famous mac and cheese." Mac ate a big forkful. "Didn't you hear? Your bar has the best food in all of Boston."

"Oh really?" McKenna sat down on a barstool beside Mac. "Although I know our food is better than the average bar, I could have sworn you were here so early because Mom called to tell you about her engagement."

Mac didn't answer and continued eating her mac and cheese.

"Mac, I've met him and he isn't like the others. I think you'd like him."

Mac groaned. "Then why don't you come with me?"

"I've already hung out with Mom and Rick several times. It's your turn and I can't leave the bar this weekend."

Mac pushed aside her bowl. "This will be her sixth husband! There should be a rule against this sort of thing."

"There's no rule against following your heart," McKenna said. "I agree that Mom has been married quite a bit, but Rick is different. He really cares about her and I think he may be in it for the long haul."

"Long haul? Mom's never had the best taste in men. Neither has dad with women. Face it sis, our parents are addicted to love."

Although Mac loved her mother, Marlene Cannon could win a Pulitzer for choosing bad men. And her father, Ike, wasn't any better. Although he was only on wife number three, he'd been engaged five times.

"That's not fair, Mac. At least they aren't afraid to fall in love."

Mac huffed. "If that was a crack at me, then you can save it. I'm not afraid to fall in love. I just prefer not to waste my time on a relationship that was doomed from the start. Husbands are overrated and men are all dogs."

McKenna's eyes softened. "What about that guy you met at Ava's wedding? The one you ditched all of us for, for the rest of the night? Alexander Carter, right?"

Mac started playing with the straw of her untouched water. "What about him?"

"Nothing really," McKenna said. "I just thought that maybe there was something between you that was more than just sex."

Not just sex, but the best sex of my life. "Not sure why you thought that. We didn't even exchange numbers or anything and I left the next morning after we had sex."

"I know you did. I remember when you came back to the room. But I also distinctly remember how elated you looked when you walked in."

"Duh, sis! Good sex will do that to you. Has it been that long since you got laid?" Mac poked at her sister's side teasingly.

"You already know owning my own bar takes most of my time, but don't change the subject. When you'd come in, you told me that after you'd had sex, you spent the rest of the night talking into the wee hours of the morning. That must count for something. From what Ava told us, Alex is a good guy. The type of man you marry."

Exactly. And that spelled trouble. "I suppose. But I'm not looking for marriage. You already know that no good can come from it. Marriage isn't about love and happiness. It's about selling your soul to—"

"The devil himself. I know, I know." McKenna rolled her eyes. "Despite your negative views, didn't you make a pact with your friends to get married in a year?"

"What does that have to do with anything?"

"It has everything to do with it. How can you dislike the idea of marriage when you made a pact to do the very thing you despise? I know how you are Mac. As soon as a relationship starts to get serious, you bolt. And when it comes to your friends, you like to be first at everything."

"And I plan to be the first at this too," Mac said with a laugh as she stood to leave. "There is no way any of the ladies are beating me to the alter. I already have a bullet proof plan in place."

McKenna squinted her eyes. "That doesn't sound good. What exactly is your plan Mac?"

When Mac reached for her purse, her stance faltered and she reached out her hand to grip the nearby stool. Unfortunately, she gripped Frank's shoulder instead, causing him to spill some of his drink.

"Dang, sweet stuff. All you had to do was ask. Of course, I'll marry you." He leaned in for a kiss.

"Eww, get away." She pushed away from Frank and sat back down on the stool she'd just vacated. Mac pulled out her small teal book from her purse and shuffled to a couple pages in the middle that had five names listed.

"What's that?" McKenna asked when Mac waved the pages in front of her face. "It's not your regular black book."

"Nope, it isn't," Mac said with a smile. "I ditched my black book and upgraded to teal. This book is the reason why I will be the first to complete the pact and win the best friend challenge."

McKenna glanced over the names. "I'm almost afraid to ask, but am I to assume that one of these five men are your future husband?"

"You guessed it sis! I've had previous relationships with each of these men, but we knew that love and marriage wasn't in our cards. So instead, we made business agreements so that—." Mac's voice trailed off when McKenna plopped her face down on the counter of the bar.

"Please tell me you're joking," McKenna said as she lifted her head.

Mac blinked rapidly. "Joking about what?"

"Mac, please tell me that you don't have a list of men that will agree to marry you for business purposes."

"Fine." Mac closed her book and placed it back in her purse. "I won't tell you, although I'm sure you know you're right. I do have contracts with these five men for situations such as this."

"Sis, you can't be serious. Do I even want to ask how you got five men to sign business marriage contracts?"

Mac shrugged. "It was easy, really. All they really signed was an agreement stating they were interested. The contract comes if we go through with it. They feel the same way I do about marriage, but we realize that sometimes, a spouse is needed to further a career."

"And how exactly does this qualify? It's a pact you made with your friends. Surely, they won't agree when they won't get anything out of it."

"You're right." Mac scrunched her forehead in thought. "What am I going to do?"

McKenna rubbed her shoulder. "Just tell the girls the truth. They'll understand."

Mac whipped her head to her sister. "Hell no! That's not what I meant. I meant to say that I need to figure out what I can do to make the idea appeal to them, but make no mistake, I'm going through with this. You know I don't back out of a bet. Especially a best friend challenge. They already think I won't go through with it."

"That's because your friends know you," McKenna said with a laugh. "Quinn started a poll to see how long it would take you to back out. I said one week, so I already lost my money."

"Did ya'll really place bets on my love life?"

"Not your love life, sis. We placed bets on you backing out of the pact."

"It doesn't matter." Mac took a swig of her water. "I don't plan on backing out, and one way or another, I'm going to be married first." Mac thought about her five prospects. "I'm sure I can spark enough interest to convince one of these lucky hopefuls to take me off the market. I just need to see which of these men has a business need that I can help fulfill. That way, they get something out of this merger."

"Are you listening to yourself?" McKenna asked. "So, you're not going to marry for love?"

"Girl, please. Love is for suckers. This will be nothing more than a business agreement. Quinn never laid out any rules, so in my mind, I'm not breaking any."

McKenna shook her head. "And I assume after you've fulfilled the pact, you'll just..."

"Get a divorce," Mac finished. "Just like most of the human population."

"Sis, you never cease to surprise me." McKenna rose from her seat. "This should be interesting."

* * *

"THAT CONCLUDES OUR MEETING," Alex said as he disconnected his laptop from the monitor. "Shane will be able to answer any questions you may have about the Camplen project."

"I actually have something to say that's not related to the project," said Pete, Senior Project Development Manager.

"Shoot."

Pete looked at a few others hesitantly before standing. "Well, in honor of your birthday that was a few days ago, the staff wanted to get you a late present."

Alex clenched his jaw in preparation. Ever since he'd taken the role as CEO two years ago, he'd learned that any time his staff looked around nervously, he probably wasn't going to like where the conversation was headed. Especially Pete. They'd been friends for years, but Alex hadn't really hung out with him in a while.

"We know you don't like celebrating birthdays," Pete said, "but we all chipped in to get you a gift." Pete handed him a sealed envelope. As Alex apprehensively opened it, he looked toward his brother who was Senior Vice President and had a closer relationship with the staff than he did. Shane shrugged, indicating that he was unaware of what was inside the envelop.

When he finally pulled out the sheet of paper, he was relieved until he read the details on the sheet. "Two-week consultation with an interior decorator?" Alex looked from Pete to the rest of the staff. "Is this your way of telling me you don't like the decor in my home?"

Alex had hosted a gathering some weeks ago, but no one had mentioned that they didn't care for his décor.

"No, it's not that," Pete said. "However you decorate your house is your business. This gift is for the office."

Alex raised an eyebrow. "The office?"

"Yes, the office. We know it's not in the budget this year to hire any outside assistance, so we all chipped in for this. My wife knows the designer, so she gave us a good rate."

Alex glanced around the room again. "So you guys want me to redecorate my office?"

"Not just your office," said Lydia, the Director of Operations. "The entire firm needs a redesign and we figured that we would help the process along."

Alex stared from his staff to the piece of paper. He caught the underlining meaning of what they were trying to say. "Thank you," he said to the group. "I appreciate this."

He watched those around the conference table break out into slow smiles before they all stood to leave.

"Listen, man, I know you don't like being cornered," Pete said when only the two of them and Shane remained in the conference room. "Everyone really thinks you're a great CEO, but morale is down and you know as well as I do that it's time to move on."

"I'm not thinking about Kimberly." Alex frowned, annoyed that he'd even voiced her name aloud. Not only was Kimberly his ex, but it was after that relationship that he'd decided to take a break from dating and focus on his career.

"Yeah, I know," Pete said. "We're all close at this firm, so we're just worried about you. A redesign will do this office some good and boost morale. Plus, it's looked the same for years, so a change would be good."

Alex thought about his mentor and friend, Pat Marx, who'd started the environmental engineer firm from scratch and had left him in charge to continue the legacy.

"Pat said something similar to me last week when we talked." Alex clasped his hands together. "All right, I'll have my assistant reach out to the designer this week."

"Sounds good," Pete said, clasping him on his back.

As Alex returned to his office, he didn't miss the excitement in his staff's eyes. Marx Engineering really did employ a good group of people and he was glad that they cared about his well-being enough to pay their own money when a change was needed.

"Hey, Sharon," he said to his assistant. "Can you make sure that the entire staff gets an end-of-the season bonus this month?"

"Will they get a holiday bonus, too?" Sharon asked.

"Of course."

Sharon shook her head. "I don't think we have two bonuses in the budget."

"No worries," Alex said. "I'll personally cover the seasonal bonuses. Just work it out with that separate account I keep for rainy days."

Sharon smile. "Will do."

Once Alex was back in his office, he did something he'd been doing more times than he could count in the past few weeks. He opened his wallet and pulled out a small piece of paper.

"Sexy siren," he whispered as he smoothed his fingers over the red lip imprint. To date, he'd only broken his vow of celibacy for one woman and one woman only.

Mackenzie Cannon.

Although he'd known it would only be for one night, the time he'd spent with her had been one of the best experiences he'd ever had. Sure, the sex had been amazing, but it hadn't only been about that. They'd talked for hours after about things he rarely discussed with someone he barely knew. They only time they'd taken a break from talking was to stop and have sex again.

He'd had every intention on continuing their intimate connection in the morning, but he'd awaken to find her gone and only a piece of paper with a kiss on it in her wake.

It didn't take a genius to figure out that Mac preferred keeping men at arm's length. Owen had told him that much the next morning since apparently, everyone had seen them leave the wedding reception together.

However, knowing that Mac didn't do relationships hadn't made him think about her any less.

"Get over it, Alex," he said aloud to himself. Despite how close he was to his college buddy, Owen, he doubted he would see Mac again unless Owen and Ava decided to through a party in their hometown and both he and Mac happened to make it. Since Alex barely took time off from work, odds were that he wouldn't be seeing her anytime soon, so even though she often appeared in his daydreams, it would suit him well to try and focus on something else. Like the numbers he had to crunch before leaving for the day.

CHAPTER 2

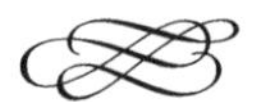

"You can do this," Mac said to herself as she got off the ferry and walked into the direction of the chic Boston restaurant. It wasn't that she didn't want to see her mom. Quite the opposite. Mac hadn't seen her mother in a few weeks, so she was looking forward to seeing her. However, she wasn't looking forward to meeting her mother's new fiancé.

"How may I help you?" the hostess said.

"Hello. I'm looking for the table of Marlene Cannon."

"Sure. Right this way."

Mac followed the hostess to the table where her mother was seated with her latest conquest. Her mom spotted her before she made it to the table.

"Mackenzie, sweetie, I'm so glad you could make it."

Growing up, friends and classmates had shortened her name to Mac, but her mother was the only one who still called her Mackenzie.

"Hi, Mom," Mac said, leaning down to hug her mom. Her eyes ventured to the good-looking man with silver hair and beard. *At least Mom has good taste.*

"Mackenzie, this is Rick, my one true love. Rick, this is my oldest daughter, Mackenzie."

"It's nice to meet you," Rick said as he extended a hand. "Your mother has told me so much about you."

"I wish I could say the same," Mac said honestly as she took a seat at the table.

"Mackenzie, enough of that."

"It's fine," Rick said. "I understand your concern, Mackenzie."

"Mac," she corrected him.

"Okay, I understand your concern, Mac, but I assure you that I adore your mother and my only wish is to make her as happy as she's made me. She's enriched my life in ways I never thought possible."

Mac squinted her eyes in observation. "And why should I believe you?"

"Mackenzie," her mother warned again.

"I don't expect you to take my word for it," Rick said. "But I'm hoping that the more you get to know me, you will see this through my actions."

Mac's eyes ventured to Rick's hand as he lifted her mom's hand and placed it in his own. *Innocent until proven guilty.* The motto didn't really apply to Rick since he hadn't done anything wrong, but Mac needed to adapt the motto to the situation. She didn't want to see her mom get hurt again.

"My sister told me good things about you," Mac said, extending an olive branch. "And if McKenna says you're good people, then I believe her."

"Thank you, Mac." Rick smiled, but his smile was nothing compared to her mom's mega-watt grin.

"You're welcome," Mac said as the waiter approached to take their orders.

"So, Rick. Do you work?" she asked after the waiter left.

"I'm retired and doing everything I can to make this little lady happy." Rick kissed Marlene's cheek.

Laying it on a little thick, mister. "Aww," Mac said, trying her best not to clench her teeth. "How sweet."

"He's the sweetest man I've ever met," Marlene said, nuzzling her nose in his neck.

"I'm only sweet because you make me a better man."

"No," Marlene said. "You're sweet because you are an amazing man."

"It's all you, dumpling," he said. "All you."

Lawd help me get through this dinner. Mac's drink hadn't arrived yet, so she downed her mom's wine instead. As predicted, her mother was wearing her Rick goggles and didn't even notice.

"Rick, do you have any kids?" Mac asked, trying to get their attention.

"No," Rick said. "But I'm looking forward to having you and McKenna in my life."

"Oh, Rick," Marlene said. "The girls are excited to have you, too, aren't you, Mackenzie?"

"So excited," Mac lied. "I can't believe my mom has found love again." She tried to hide the hint of sarcasm in her voice, but it slipped out before she could catch it. Instead of reprimanding her, her mom just rolled her eyes.

Maybe ask a question that won't result in me gagging or my mom getting on my case. "How did you both spend your day?" she asked. She'd known they were hanging out together before dinner.

"It was wonderful," Marlene said. "Rick took me fishing. Then we took the ferry to one of the islands for a short hike."

"Really?" Mac asked when her drink finally arrived. "You hate anything outdoors."

"Not anymore," Marlene said as she smiled at Rick. "He helped me realize that the only reason I didn't enjoy the outdoors was because I never had anyone take the time to make sure I enjoyed it. Rick opened my eyes to an entirely new experience."

Rick stared into Marlene's eyes. "Sweet stuff, the minute I met you, my eyes were opened to a new experience as well. I'm only returning the favor."

Marlene lifted Rick's face to hers. "Stud muffin, you can return the favor to me anytime," she said before placing a sweet kiss on his lips. After a couple seconds, Marlene and Rick entered a serious lip lock.

Seriously! "Another drink, please," Mac said to the waiter when he passed by the table. "Mom, can you and Rick try and keep your hands off one another until after we eat?" Her request fell on deaf ears.

Breaking up a good kiss is like waking someone up from sleep walking. If you get slapped in the face, you only have yourself to blame. "I know, Grandma Pearl," Mac whispered to herself as she thought about her grandma's warning. However, even though she wasn't going to break up the kiss, it didn't mean she had to witness it any longer.

"I'll be back," she said, standing from the table. "Bathroom break." On her way to the bathroom, she briefly thought about heading to the front door and walking out, but she knew it would cause World War III with her mother.

She turned back to her mom and Rick and noticed that they'd also gotten the attention of patrons dining at nearby tables. Although she wasn't too fond of her mother getting married for a sixth time, she had to admire the fact that no matter what Marlene Cannon did, she *never* apologized for being anyone but herself.

Glad Mom passed that trait down. Mac was constantly telling her friends that she couldn't apologize for being her. It's not that they asked. She just felt like supplying the information. And right now, what Mac needed was to ignore the situation with her mom and Rick.

When she got to the bathroom, she shuffled through her purse and pulled out her little teal book. She knew it was old school to have her fuck buddies written down in a book as opposed to her cell phone, but she didn't care.

She came to Alexander Carter's name and sighed. Not only was he the best sex she'd ever had, but the man had the body of a Greek god. Mac wasn't one to drool, but he'd been a work of art, sculpted in lean muscle dipped in dark chocolate. One night with him had taken Mac's wet fantasies from rated R, to Adult Only.

You'll never ride that bull again. And truthfully, she hadn't even gotten a chance to ride him then. It wasn't that she regretted her decision to leave him before he'd awakened, but right now, she would give her right arm to get another taste of that delicious, robust coffee. Too bad she only had his name written down. No number. No location. Sure, she could get that information from Ava, but sometimes, a one night stand was meant to stay a one night stand.

As much as she hated to admit it, with Alex it hadn't only been about the sex. The conversations they had in-between their sexy rendezvous' had been refreshing. It had been entirely too long since Mac had enjoyed talking to a man on a deeper level. She typically preferred the Let's Flirt Than Fuck mentality when it came to the opposite sex and as unhealthy as that sounded, it worked for her.

She may not be able to get him off her mind, but there was no way she was reaching out to Ava about him. He would stay a part of her past… No matter how many countless orgasms she'd had that night.

* * *

"Crap, can anything else go wrong today," Alex said as he grabbed a roll of paper towels from his drawer and started dabbing the important documents on his desk.

Alex's day had started off badly and was gradually getting worse by the second. After staying up all night, he'd needed four cups of coffee just to make it through his important meetings. Problem was, two cups was his limit because anything over that made him feel jittery. By the third cup, he'd convinced himself that one more wouldn't hurt.

Not only had he possibly lost a big client today, but things had progressively gone downhill when one of his top assistant project managers announced that he was quitting to go work for the competition. Since they didn't want to risk him stealing any information, Alex had to make him pack his things and leave immediately. He'd only been gone a few hours and already, most of the remaining PM's were complaining about the work load he'd left.

If there was such a word for the type of day he'd had, it would probably fit somewhere in-between *fucked-up* and *hellish.*

On days like today, I really need a sexual release. Alex shook his head at the direction of his thoughts. Masturbating could only get you so far. What he needed was some good old-fashioned fucking and there was only one woman who came to mind.

Don't think about her, Alex. The problem with thinking about Mackenzie Cannon was that he wouldn't be able to stop thinking about her once his brain cells started pulling epic sex scenes from his memories. After he started down that road, he would get aroused. Once he was aroused, he'd eventually get blue balls and no man wanted blue balls. Especially when they were still at the office.

He'd just finished cleaning up the spilled coffee when there was a knock on his door. He glanced at the clock and noticed it was after-hours and his assistant Sharon was probably gone.

"Come in," he said.

"Hey, man, did you forget about your six p.m.?"

Alex turned to Pete. "I don't have any additional client meetings today."

"Not a client," Pete said. "A meeting with the interior decorator."

Shit. He'd forgotten and, quite frankly, he didn't have time for it.

"Is the interior decorator here?"

"Yeah, she's in the lobby."

"Okay," Alex said. "I'll get her."

"No worries, I'll bring her to your office."

Alex was just tossing the last of the coffee stained paper towels when he heard a seductive voice drift to his ears.

"Alexander Carter is the CEO," she said in what he assumed was supposed to be a low voice, but Alex had excellent hearing. He didn't make it a habit to eavesdrop on people's conversations, but he couldn't help it that he had the hearing of an elephant. Nor could he ignore the distressed sound in her voice.

"Yes, he is," Pete responded. "What's the problem?"

"So much," she said. "I can't do this project."

Can't do this project? Alex walked closer to the entrance of his open door, careful not to make his presence known as he listened to the hallway conversation.

"What do you mean, you can't do it?" Pete asked. "We already presented it to him. We can't take back the gift."

"Then find someone else," she said. "Because there is no way in hell I'm doing it. Maybe I'll send one of my employees."

"You're the best," Pete said. "I don't know what's going on, but Alex is a good guy."

"I'm sure he is, but you need to find someone else to help Mr. Carter."

Alex wasn't sure if it was the silky tones in her voice or the way she'd said *Mr. Carter*. Either way, he stepped into the hallway just as she was walking away.

"Mac, wait," he said.

The woman stopped in her tracks and slowly turned her head over her shoulder. *It* is *her.* She hadn't even fully turned around, but he'd know that ass anywhere. Hell, he'd spent a better part of the night they'd had sex cupping it, biting it, squeezing it. Doing anything she'd allow him to do to it really.

"Hey," she said in a chipped tone. "I wasn't aware that you were the CEO of this firm."

Alex smirked. "I wasn't aware that you were the interior decorator."

"Interior decorator," she said. "I'm a Feng-Shui consultant."

"A Feng-what?"

She rolled her eyes. "A Feng-Shui consultant. Although interior decorating comes with the job, that's not what I am."

"My apologies," Alex said. "I didn't know."

Mac turned to Pete. "Pete, why does he not know what I do?"

"Um." Pete looked from one to the other. "Do you two know each other?"

"Yes," Alex said at the same time that Mac said no.

"Um, okay." Pete glanced at both of them again. "Well, Mac, we didn't mention your title because we knew Alex wouldn't understand it and we felt it best that you explain it to him. And, Alex, Mac is successful at what she does and as you know, she's a friend of my wife and I."

Alex was listening to Pete, but he was more so enjoying the way Mac had her arms crossed defensively over her chest. Even when she was annoyed, she was still sexy as hell.

"It's nice to see you again," Alex said, ignoring the fact that Pete was still talking.

She gave him a forced smile. "Wish I could say the same."

"You could," he said as a matter-of-factly. "I think you do, you just don't want to vocalize it."

She shrugged. "Nope, can't say that I do."

He wondered if she knew that whenever she was uncomfortable, her tell-tale sign was the way she would tilt her head to the side and bite the lower right corner of her lip. While they'd talked the night they were together, she'd done that numerous times throughout their conversation. The move was sexy as hell, and surprisingly, she'd pushed through her discomfort. *Just like she probably will now.*

Pete clasped his hands together. "Well, since you two obviously know one another, I'm going to get home to my beautiful wife and leave you both to talk."

"Is anyone else in the office?" Alex asked, his eyes still planted on Mac.

"Nope, so you can lock up when you leave." Pete turned to Mac. "You okay?"

Although she seemed to be debating what she would tell Pete, she eventually nodded and said that she was fine.

"Care to join me in my office so we can discuss business?" Alex suggested once they were alone.

She hesitated for a few seconds before responding. "Sure."

Once they got to the office, instead of sitting across from him at his desk, she took a seat on the other side of the room on his sofa.

So this is what we're doing, he thought. The woman who'd approached him at the bar a couple months ago was bold, confident. She was upfront about what she wanted and when she wanted it. The Mac he was meeting today wasn't the same. She was reserved. Distant. It wasn't that he needed her to be the same Mac, but he'd be lying if he didn't admit that he particularly missed the siren he'd met at their friend's wedding.

Even so, she looked just as gorgeous as he'd remembered. Tonight, she was wearing a white blouse with the top two buttons undone revealing the peak of a black lace bra. His eyes ventured to her hips that were covered in a black pencil skirt and feet adorned in red stilettos that served as a reminder of how beautiful her feet were. He shook his head when he remembered how she'd squirmed when he'd massaged her feet before sucking her toes.

Mac shifted in her seat under his observant gaze. The gentleman thing to do would be to stop looking at her as if she were an ice cream cone on a hot summer day and talk business.

Unfortunately for her, his eyes couldn't stay off of the way her plump ass cheeks looked while she was sitting on his sofa. When a woman had a small butt, she could sit down with no problem. However, when a woman had an ass like Mac, she had to sit a little on the side of her hip to account for the round piece of meat she was packing. Alex didn't know if Mac remembered all the attention he'd given her butt, but there was nothing he liked more than a juicy backside.

"So, I'm really intrigued to learn more about what you do," he said as he stopped his perusal of her and pulled up a chair to sit across from her. He was willing to give her some space, but not *that* much space.

"I'm a Feng-Shui consultant, which means, I specialize in ensuring that your environment and everything surrounding your environment is harmonized. The term Feng-Shui is an ancient art and physiological system that was developed in China over three-thousand years ago. The whole idea behind Feng-Shui is that based off your surroundings and environment, it can result in good energy or bad energy either spiritually, creatively, and even through love, money and health. It affects all aspects of life, so my job is to take one's environment and apply Feng-Shui methods to your home or office space to assist in your harmonious journey."

Alex hoped that he wasn't looking at Mac as if she had two heads, but he was pretty sure he looked like a deer caught in head-lights. It's not that he wasn't thoroughly impressed by what she was saying because he was. However, he was caught off guard by what she did for a living. Based off their first meeting, he wouldn't take her for the harmonious energy type. *You would if you thought about the conversations you had with her* after *sex.*

It was true that he hadn't expected to connect with her on a deeper level after they'd had sex, but that's exactly what had happened.

"Feng-Shui sounds very intriguing," he said. "Much like the woman explaining it."

"Thank you." Mac briefly diverted her attention to the ceiling. "Hence the reason I'm here. I'm friends with Pete's wife, Sarah, and when I was having dinner with the two of them a couple weeks ago, they asked me if I would be willing to assist a friend who needed my intimate services." Her eyes grew big. "I meant my work services."

"I'm sure," he said. "Although, I wasn't aware that any other services were up for grabs."

"They aren't," she said sternly. "Getting back to what I was saying, Pete never told me who my consulting services were for and I've been pretty busy these past few weeks, so I didn't ask too many questions. I didn't even find out the address for tonight's meeting until an hour ago."

"Are you dating anyone?" Alex asked.

She studied his eyes. "Why do you ask?"

"I'd think it was obvious," he said, leaning his elbows on his knees so that he was closer to her.

"Um, I think we should keep whatever happened in the past, in the past. I'm only here to consult on your office space."

"Not my office as well as my home?" he asked.

"No, just your office."

"I thought you mentioned that Feng-Shui was about harmonizing the energy in an office and home. I need a lot of help in that area, so why not assist with both?"

Mac frowned. "Because it's not necessary. After two weeks, you'll be able to take everything you've learned about harmonizing your office and adapt that to your home environment."

The Mac he'd met at their friend's wedding had spoken in a smooth, velvety voice. The Mac he was witnessing tonight was talking faster than normal. *Is she nervous around me?*

"Are you scared to be alone with me in my home?" he asked out of curiosity and concern. Her eyes flew to his.

"I'm not scared of anything," she said. If he hadn't been

watching her so closely, he would have missed the look of challenge that flashed in her eyes.

She stood and outreached her hand. "Okay, Alex. If you want my consulting services for your office and home then I'll oblige you. But, remember, it's my rules. You have to promise to be open and willing to accept the changes I suggest."

"Deal," he said without hesitation. As he accepted her handshake, he tried not to be too disappointed that she'd called him Alex and not Mr. Carter.

In due time, he reminded himself. *No, wait. You're supposed to be celibate again. You shouldn't be thinking about having a repeat performance with Mac.*

"Is that all?" she asked.

Hell no, that's not all. You squirming on my sofa as I get reacquainted with your delicious, sweet taste is the only thing that would satisfy me until you leave.

"That's all," he said instead. She lifted an eyebrow, but didn't say anything else.

"Then I guess I'll see you tomorrow." She reached into her purse and pulled out her cell phone. "What's your home address?"

Now it was his turn to look surprised. "You're starting with my home first?"

"Yeah. Since I'll be consulting on your home and office, I usually like to start with the home in these cases. Do you have a problem with that?"

He smiled slyly. "Not at all." As he rattled off his address and escorted her to the door, he couldn't help but smile at the turn of events that suddenly made this the best day he'd had in months. Mac didn't seem too thrilled to discover that he was her client, but Alex planned on making the most of their time together.

CHAPTER 3

This is stupid. Just tell him that you've come down with the flu and have to reschedule. Mac shook her head at the thought. Rescheduling with Alex meant that she'd have to prolong her two weeks that she had to work with him.

She'd been standing outside the door of his home for ten minutes and was no sooner ready to knock on the door than she had been when she'd initially arrived. She took a deep breath.

Mac had always been a confident person, but running into Alex was throwing off her entire equilibrium. There weren't many things that caught Mac off guard, but unknowingly walking into Alex's company and realizing that he was the client she was supposed to work with was doing crazy things to her nerves. For example, exhibit A. *Why in the ever-living hell am I not knocking on the door already?* She'd been dreading this meeting since she was at his office yesterday. Any woman in her position would be just as apprehensive, right? Mac had spent her entire life avoiding men like Alex for one reason and one reason only... *Love.*

Alex had *I'm The Type of Man You Fall in Love With* written all over his handsome features and Mac knew that love wasn't in her future. Too many times, she'd seen her parents hurt by love and unfortunately, it hadn't just stopped at them. How many times had she witnessed one of her mom's friends crying over a husband who'd left her or cheated on her with another woman? How many times had Mac witnessed her own mother cry buckets of tears after realizing that she was in yet another failed marriage? How many times had she witnessed her father break a woman's heart except for the one time that her mother broke his? *And don't forget when your heart was ripped in two by a man you thought loved you as much as you loved him.* She could still taste the bitterness in her mouth from her own failed relationship with her ex years ago.

Bottom line… She'd seen love fail one too many times. Sure, Ava and Owen looked nauseatingly happy on their wedding day, but how long could that last? Almost every relationship that Mac had observed in her lifetime proved that love wasn't worth the risk. Mac may be a risk taker in every sense of the word, but she drew a big bold fat line through love.

As she studied the closed door, she took a deep breath. *You'll be fine, Mac. You know Alex. You've had sex with Alex. Therefore, you know how to handle Alex.*

As a matter of fact, men didn't handle Mac, Mac handled men. So good that other women often asked her how she did it. "That's right. You can handle this," she said as she finally knocked on the door.

A few seconds later, Alex opened the door looking sexier than she'd ever seen him look before. His hair and goatee looked freshly cut. His eyes were bright and warm. Instead of a tux or suit—birthday or otherwise—like the previous times she'd seen him, navy blue jogging pants hung low on his hips and a white sleeveless tank showed his muscular arms and delectable abs. She briefly closed her eyes as she thought about the way her tongue had dipped into each crevice of those abs to suck up the wine she'd poured on them.

"Glad you finally knocked," he said.

She opened her eyes. "What do you mean?"

He pointed upward to the corner of his porch. She cringed when her eyes landed on a camera.

"You were watching me the entire time?"

"Only because I happened to pass by my security room and saw your beautiful face cross the screen."

"That's creepy," she said.

"No," he said. "Creepy would be if I hadn't told you at all, then let you in my home and didn't inform you that there are two more cameras inside. One that faces the foyer and front hallway and another on the second level in the hall."

Mac shook her head. "One, why in the world do you have a security room and so many cameras? Two, why do you think it's okay to watch people when they don't know it?"

"Although I'm not into material things, I have a lot of valuable belongings," he said. "Plus, it's my house. My porch. My cameras. My choice."

Mac rolled her eyes. *What I'd give to wipe that smug look off his face.*

"Oh, I have a few suggestions about that, but I figured you wanted to focus on business first."

"I didn't even say anything," she said.

"You didn't have to." He winked. "Please, come in." He stepped aside and allowed her to walk past him. She purposely held her breath as she did, so that she wouldn't breathe in his enticing scent.

Luckily, she was immediately distracted by the beauty of his home. Everything was relatively clean, and even at a first glance, she could tell that each item had a place where it belonged. Either Alex had cleaned for her benefit or he kept an extremely clean living environment. She had a feeling it was the latter.

"Your home is beautiful, but I already see a few things that need to be changed," she said as she walked from the living room to the dining room.

"Like what?"

"Well, for starters, part of your house is contemporary, while the other part is country chic. Are you from Boston?"

"No," he said. "I'm originally from Texas, why?"

I knew it, she thought. It wasn't until she was in his office that she'd realized he had a sort of southern twang in his voice that mixed with a city accent. She had the same since she grew up in South Carolina and now lived in Boston, so she'd recognized it immediately. She'd also noticed that neither of them had that Boston blend.

"Although your home looks amazing, your styles and tastes are competing with each other," she said. "Each room has a barn door as opposed to a regular door, but instead of wooden furniture to accentuate the style, you have metal or steel material for your table and some furniture, but not brick or another complimenting material."

Alex glanced around the room before his eyes landed back on Mac. "Is there something wrong with that?"

"No, there isn't. It's just that most people who have decorations like yours, are still trying to figure out their exact place in the world. They are holding onto their past roots, trying to grow present roots, and apprehensive with where they should plant future roots. Therefore, those indecisions are reflected in their interior decorations. Now, some of this can be personal style, but with others, it's a reflection of their life and the everyday struggles they go through to try and find something that fits."

Mac glanced at Alex in time to see him slightly flinch at her words. *Hmm, I must be close to the truth.*

"You weren't lying when you said you were good at what you do."

"I've been known to help a few hundred in this area," she said with a smile. They walked around the rest of the lower level. "And be prepared to bring in more color."

"More color?" Alex asked. "Like, what colors? Not super bright colors I hope."

"Maybe, maybe not. You said you'd be open."

"I am open," he said. "I just don't want my home looking tacky."

"It won't." Mac placed her hand on his forearm. "Adding a few bursts of red or green will do your home's palate some good. Don't worry, I have you covered."

Alex lifted an eyebrow.

"I meant *it*," she said. "I have *it* covered, not you." She immediately dropped her hand to her side, ignoring the smirk on Alex's face.

When she walked towards the fireplace, an object on the mantel immediately caught her eye. "Wow, this piece is amazing. It's so intricate and one of the few splashes of color in your home."

"That's one of my favorite pieces," Alex said as he placed both hands in the pockets of his jogging pants. "I got it when I was backpacking through East Africa a few years ago. While I was in a small village, a matriarch of one of the families gave this to me as a gift. I'm sure she could have made a lot of money on it, so I didn't want to take it, but she insisted."

"This is an amazing gift," Mac said as she continued to admire the blue, gold and turquoise design on the vase. "You must have made a great first impression."

"I spent a year helping different African villages clean their water supply and better their environment so that they could continue to grow their own vegetation. I received a lot of uniquely special gifts such as this vase on my travels and each gift holds a special place in my heart. But I wasn't the one who made an impression on them. They were the ones who made an impression on me."

Mac smiled. *He just keeps on surprising me.* "Did you travel through your company or did you decide to help the villages on your own?"

"Originally, I had gone to Africa for work, but on journey to my flight back, we passed so many places that needed clean water supply and soil to plant seeds. My heart couldn't let me return to the States without helping at least one village. My brother shared my same desire to help and so did eight more staff members. Soon, what started as a two-week project turned into a twelve-month goal to help as many as we could."

Mac studied his eyes, certain that Alex had no idea how much his words warmed her heart. "You stayed behind, didn't you?"

"What do you mean?" he asked.

"I assume that your company couldn't afford for ten people to be gone for long since I'm sure you were winning bids for other contracts. So, I was thinking that you were probably the only one who stayed the entire twelve months?"

"I was," Alex said. "It was before I became CEO, but I was taking a risk being gone that long. Luckily, the previous CEO understood my desire to help and allowed me to take that year off." He squinted. "How'd you guess that?"

Hmm... How did I guess that? The answer was right at the tip of her tongue, but she knew if she said it aloud, it would show more cards than she wanted Alex to see. "I guess I knew it was the case because it's easy to tell you're a selfless man. You want what's best for those around you. The fact that you couldn't leave Africa without helping people further proves the content of your character. I'm sure you spent a lot of personal money to clean the water supply and purchase soil, but I also wouldn't be surprised if you continue to send money to those villages that you helped."

His eyes widened. "You're very intuitive," he said, indirectly confirming her assumption. "Although I could call you the same thing."

"What do you mean?"

He smiled. "I could call you selfless as well."

Mac laughed. "Although I don't think I'm a selfish person, selfless is not exactly what most people would use to describe me."

"I'm not most people," Alex said with a shrug. "And anyone who can choose a less-fortunate family every year, give their home a complete make-over, and front the entire bill is definitely selfless in my mind."

Mac's lips parted. "How did you know that?"

"Well, I may have researched your company after our meeting yesterday," Alex said as he shuffled from one foot to the other. "Then watched the news special that was done on your business a couple years ago."

"I help families make their living quarters feel more like a home, but it's hardly the same thing. What you do makes a big difference."

Alex laughed. "And what you do doesn't?"

"It does," Mac said. "At least I think it does. When I first started my business – long before I had an actual office and employees – I knew I wanted to help people turn their houses into warm homes. The first time I witnessed an entire family cry after the make-over was the most rewarding feeling I'd ever had."

"I'm sure it was." Alex stepped closer to her. "When we first met, you said that you understood my desire to want to have solid roots in a location and you mentioned moving around a lot and Rosewood Heights being the only place that felt like home. You make-over homes to help at least one family every year not go through the same instability you felt, don't you?"

"How did you..." Mac's voice trailed off as she stared into Alex's eyes. There was no point in finishing her question by asking how he'd guessed that. She assumed it was the same way she knew certain things about him even if he didn't say it.

"Yes, that definitely plays a part in my desire to help families by using my expertise."

"You surprise me," Alex said, his voice throatier than before.

"You surprise me too." At her words, he stepped even closer. Every warning bell in her body went off at his closeness. *Remember, this is a business meeting.* In all honesty, she could stand there and gaze into his almost-black eyes all night. *Wait, what? You're here to Feng-Shui his home, not gaze into his eyes all night.*

"Well, then." Mac cleared her throat and took a step back from Alex. "I think we should get back focused. Care to show me upstairs?"

For a second, she thought he didn't hear her since he was still hypnotizing her with his eyes. "Sure," he finally said with a sly smile. "Let me just go wake up Daisy first. She's in my bedroom asleep."

Say what? If Mac had been drinking water, she would have spit it across the entire hardwood floor.

"Um, Daisy? There's a Daisy here?" Mac tried to talk in her calmest voice possible.

"Yeah, she's upstairs. Do you want to meet her?"

"No, not particularly."

"Come on, I'll introduce you." Before she could protest again, Alex was dragging her upstairs in the direction of a bedroom.

I can't believe he has a girlfriend. Mac was fuming, but doing her best to try and hide it. *Even worse, I can't believe I even give a shit.* It didn't take long for her to understand her knee-jerk reaction to his comment being one of jealousy. *Well this is new.* Mac couldn't remember the last time she was jealous and the situation would be comical if it were happening to anyone other than her.

Mac may not be big on relationships, but the one thing she did not like to do was share with another woman. Granted, frivolous relationships caused for some sort of non-chalantness on the whole issue, but she had standards. And right now, Alex was causing her blood pressure to rise.

Get ahold of yourself, Mac. He's not your man. He's not your fuck buddy. He's not even a friend. He's a client, and who he sleeps with is his business.

"Before I left the bed this morning, I asked her to keep it warm for me."

Oh hell no. That's it. "Alex, this is really inappropriate," she said when he opened the door to his bedroom and pulled her inside. "I think it's best if I leave." When he finally let her hand go, she went to the door.

"Mac, I'd like for you to meet Daisy. Daisy, meet my friend, Mac."

At the sound of a purr, Mac turned around. "A cat," she said, walking up to the furry animal. Mac playfully hit his shoulder. "The *she* you were referring to is your cat?"

"Yeah," Alex said with a laugh. "Figured I'd tease you to break up the sexual tension after our discussion earlier."

Mac laughed. She didn't think it was possible, but he got even sexier. She'd always considered herself more of a dog person, but there was something sexy as hell about Alex standing there, nuzzling up with a cute grey and white cat.

Not only had he succeeded in breaking the tension, but she appreciated that he'd been up front with the fact that the tension was of the sexual nature.

"It helped," she said as she rubbed Daisy's head. "And Daisy is a cutie-pie." At her words, the feline rubbed her head against Mac's cheek.

"Wow," Alex said. "Daisy never warms up to people this fast."

Mac lifted Daisy from Alex's arms and continued rubbing her. "What can I say. She knows a catch when she sees it."

It wasn't until Mac could only hear her own laughter in the room that she focused her attention back on Alex. Once she did, she wasn't surprised to find him watching her intently.

"I agree," he said in a low voice. "She knows a catch when she sees it." *Oh crap.* She knew that look in his eyes. That look of interest and awareness. She'd seen it the entire time they were together back in her hometown. She'd also seen it while she was in his office the other day. Hell, she'd seen it ten minutes prior when they were downstairs. And now, she was seeing it again.

"I was just kidding, Alex," Mac said. "My mouth is always getting me into trouble."

"I don't know about that, Mac." His eyes dropped to her lips. "I'm afraid it's your mouth that has my undivided attention."

Mac swallowed. *Jesus be a miracle.* She'd thought the ignore-and-avoid tactic would work when it came to acknowledging what had gone down between the sheets with her and Alex. However, Mac was slowly learning that it would take a miracle for them to forget or ignore what their bodies were constantly reminding them. Sexual chemistry was a beast that Mac didn't know how to slay, and the longer she stood there staring in Alex's eyes, the more unsure she was about taming the beast.

CHAPTER 4

It had been four days, eleven hours and forty-seven minutes since he'd stopped himself from stripping Mac naked in his bedroom after watching her bond so closely with Daisy.

She'd already been to his home twice more since then, but both times, she'd either had an assistant with her or someone delivering a piece of furniture or an item. Although Alex admired what Mac did for a living, he was beginning to really hate the Feng-Shui concept. All it seemed to mean was that he couldn't be alone with Mac since after that initial consultation, she always had someone with her executing her suggestions.

This evening, Mac was meeting at the office and Alex had finally come up with a solution. He knew Mac would fight him tooth and nail, but he didn't care. He had to talk to her.

"You okay, man?"

Alex looked up from his desk at his brother Shane. "I didn't even hear you come in."

"The door was cracked and I wanted to check on you. You've been pretty quiet the last few days."

Alex knew that his brother was well aware of the fact that he'd been under a lot of stress. A lot of his staff probably thought his stress had something to do with losing a contract or something else work-related, but that wasn't the case. True, work was hectic right now, but the main cause of his stress belonged to a brown-legged beauty who he couldn't stop thinking about.

He'd hoped that after five days, he would have made more progress in his relationship with Mac. He didn't want to force the situation, but it was evident that he needed to handle Mac the same way he handled business. Create a plan. Review the plan. Execute the plan. Alex hated looking at his relationship with Mac like a bid he needed to win, but he'd realized after her first night in his home that he wanted more than just a working relationship with her. He wanted whatever else Mac had to offer and if he was lucky, she was willing to date him and explore a relationship.

"Just working through things, man," Alex finally said to Shane. "I just got off the phone with that client we thought we lost, and it turns out, we got the bid."

"That's great," Shane said. "But I actually wasn't just talking about work. In the meeting I just left, Pete pulled me aside and mentioned that he hoped the staff's gift didn't backfire. What happened?"

"Nothing much," Alex said. "Except for the fact that the Feng-Shui consultant just so happens to be Mac."

Shane squinted his eyes as if trying to figure out who Mac was. He snapped his fingers the minute he figured it out. "Mac as in Mackenzie Cannon, Ava's friend? The one you slept with at the wedding?"

"I never told you we slept together."

Shane snorted. "Man, come on. You left with her and never came back to the reception. Then you had this stupid grin on your face during our entire flight home. It doesn't take a genius to figure out what happened. I'm just glad you finally got some."

"I choose to be celibate," Alex said. "Anyway, neither of us knew we'd be working together on Feng-Shuiing my house and office."

Shane gave him a blank stare. "Do I even want to know what the hell that means?"

"I'll explain it later," Alex said with a laugh. "Point is, I can't stop thinking about her and working with her is only making matters worse. Her consultation is over in about a week and I don't think I can last that long without getting some type of clarity."

"Clarity to what exactly?"

Alex put away the files he'd just looked at. "Clarity about the fact that I feel like something is happening between us, but I don't know what. What I do know, is that I want to explore it, but I'm not trying to scare her off."

"What do you mean?" Shane asked. "You can't possibly think that telling her that you're feeling her vibe and would like to get to know her better won't go over well. Women love that monogamous shit and you're a monogamous dater. You only do relationships, not casual flings."

"I hear what you're saying, but I don't think it's going to be that easy."

Shane shrugged. "You never know unless you try. She may surprise you."

Alex was about to respond, but Sharon's voice filled his intercom. "Alex, there's a Ms. Cannon here to see you."

"Okay," Alex said. "Send her in."

"And apparently, now is your chance," Shane said as he stood to leave.

Alex heard Shane greet Mac in the hallway giving him a few seconds to re-gather his thoughts after Shane's visit. *He's right, you need to just go for it.* It had been a long time since Alex had put himself out there, and although his relationship with his ex, Kimberly, had crashed and burned, he was willing to go through that same heartache again for the chance to be with a woman like Mac.

Alex had known the minute she'd approached him at the wedding that she wasn't like other women he'd met before. Within the first minutes of their initial conversation, she'd challenged him and sparked not only a physical interest, but a mental one as well. The same feeling struck him when she'd come to his home. Alex was a firm believer in the saying, beauty only goes skin deep. He needed more than good looks to attract him to a woman and the fact that Mac had piqued his interest in a short amount of time spoke volumes to Alex.

"Is this a good time?" Mac asked as she peeked her head through the cracked door.

"Now is perfect." He stood and shut the door behind her so that they could have privacy. He wasn't surprised when she went to the same couch she'd sat on before.

"Although this will be my first time getting a thorough view of your office, I brought over some Feng-Shui suggestions based off what I remember. Would you like me to dive right in?"

"No," he said and sat beside her on the couch. "I have another pressing matter I want to discuss with you first."

Her eyes looked up from her portfolio and locked with his. "What do you want to talk about?"

Damn, she's beautiful. Today, she was wearing a deep green dress that accentuated every curve of her body. Alex wasn't surprised that his dick jumped when she adjusted herself on the sofa, causing her dress to creep up her creamy brown thighs.

He wasn't sure if it was the way she tilted her head or the fact that she looked even more breathtaking than the last time he'd seen her, but he wanted—no needed—to kiss her. He was tired. Stressed. And he was looking at the one person who he knew could make it all better without even trying.

In one swift move, he slid her across the couch only more turned on by the way she gasped. As he lowered his lips to hers, he stopped mere centimeters away to give her a chance to push him away. When she didn't, he closed the distance and captured her lips in his, reconnecting with her sweet honey taste.

* * *

MAC FELT Alex's tongue slip between her lips, so she opened her mouth to accommodate him. Her hand went to the back of his neck, pulling him closer. After spending the past week thinking about him and trying to keep her distance when she saw him, she needed this. *Goodness, I've been thinking about this for days.*

Granted, she was the one who'd made sure they hadn't been alone since that first night in his home, but that didn't mean she'd hadn't been thinking about his lips every night since. Just as she'd suspected, Alex was a dangerous combination of good looks and an intelligent brain. Top that off with a selfless heart and great personality and she might as well just melt right then and there.

Maybe you could marry him and fulfill the pact? The thought entered her mind so swiftly, that she it felt like it had slapped her in the face. She almost broke their kiss, but managed to keep her lips locked to his. *Where did that thought come from?* It was one thing to give into temptation by rewarding yourself with a kiss. It was another thing entirely to want to marry a man after a few good conversations and mind-blowing sex.

But Alex makes more sense than any of your other prospects. The tiny voice on her right shoulder was really getting annoying. To dim her thoughts, she deepened the kiss, eliciting a raspy groan from Alex.

Their lips intertwined in a way that made her insides swirl in appreciation for all the wonderful things she knew he could do with his mouth.

His lips were just as she remembered. Soft, yet powerful. Demanding that she give as much as she took. She lifted her leg to get a better angle, and not before long, she was straddling him, her dress rising high on her thighs. Alex's strong hands gripped her, holding her in place as she grinded against his shaft that was straining against his pants.

"You feel amazing," he said in between kisses, squeezing her ass in a way that made her grind on him harder.

"You do, too." One would assume that based off the fact that Mac liked sex, she'd enjoy making out just as much, but that was quite the contrary. Kissing for an extended period of time had never been her thing. However, Alex was making her rethink the entire art of kissing. His expert tongue was touching a part of her that had never been touched. Or maybe, in all honesty, she'd never opened up that side of herself to be touched.

Her mom often said that she made a man work too hard to win her over. Mac had to differ. It wasn't that she made a man work too hard to win her heart. She never allowed herself to be vulnerable enough for him to do so. Although this man wasn't breaking down her walls yet, he was knocking over a few big bricks.

Over the past couple months, he'd consumed her thoughts, and she'd wondered if things would still be explosive between them if they ever saw each other again. When he did come back into her life earlier this week, she wasn't prepared for the effect he still had on her. Not only was Alex managing to ease his way back into the part of her heart that she declared off-limits, but he had a hold on her that she couldn't quite shake.

Mac adjusted her hips and his deep, appreciative groan caused her entire body to shiver. She felt the sensations build in her core as a result of the friction their bodies were causing on the most sensitive parts of her female anatomy. *You need to stop this,* she thought when she felt like she was on the brink of an orgasm. "You're in his office." Mac wasn't a virgin to being intimate in public, but she had certain rules and getting her freak on in an office wasn't something she would normally do. *But with Alex, you're learning a new kind of normal.* With Alex, he was making his own rules.

Instead of slowing down, she increased the rotation of her hips when she felt one of his hands slip underneath her dress, his thumb finding her sensitive bud of nerves.

"Ahh." She moaned into his mouth between kisses, so close she could barely stand it.

She couldn't believe she and Alex were having a full-blown make-out session with his employees just a few feet away on the other side of his office door.

The sound of her portfolio dropping had her leaping off his lap only to fall into one of the nearby chairs. Alex looked disappointed, but she needed to get a grip of herself. *You can't do that if you kept staring at his sexy and aroused self.* She pulled her dress back down and turned to close her eyes to gather her composure.

"I didn't expect for that to happen," Alex said. "But I'm glad it did. I was hoping I would get a chance to talk to you today."

"About your office Feng-Shui?"

He smiled. "Not at all." He grabbed the bottom of the chair she was sitting in and pulled it closer to him. "Firstly, can you give me one good reason why we can't continue where we left off when we were in South Carolina? Maybe even try dating?"

"I'll give you three good reasons," she said, regaining the confidence she'd had when she entered his office. "One, I'm not looking for a serious relationship. Two, I don't date my clients. And, three, unless you want to sign my fuck buddies contract, we can't take this any further."

Alex's boastful laugh was so loud, it filled the entire office. Mac glanced toward his door and noticed a couple shadowed figures, probably his staff checking to see if he was okay.

As expected, a woman's voice filled the intercom. "Sir, are you okay?"

Alex stood and walked over to his phone. "I'm fine, Sharon. Thank you."

He was still laughing when he fell back onto the couch. Mac stood over him with her arms crossed over her chest.

"Care to share what you find so funny?"

"I'm surprised you even have to ask," he said, placing his hand on his stomach as his laughter died down. "A fuck buddies contract? What exactly does that entail? And would you really make me sign it when we've already had sex?"

She frowned. "Of course, I would make you sign it. That's generally how contracts work."

"I'm a thirty-five-year-old man and I've never been asked to sign a fuck buddy's contract."

Okay, now I'm irritated. "Maybe you've never been good enough in bed for a woman to want to have a repeat performance."

"Really," he said, amusement dancing in his eyes. "Can you really say that with a straight face?"

She playfully swatted his shoulder. "There's nothing more annoying than a man with an overinflated ego."

"Ego?" he said, moving to stand in front of her. "I know a lot of men with big egos, but I'm not one of them. I wasn't trying to make fun of you, the contract just caught me off guard."

"It's not like I was offering for you to sign it," she said, trying to act unaffected by his response. *Well, that's not entirely true, but any who.* "I told you two other reasons as well."

"I know," he said. "I understand your first reason about not wanting anything serious, and although I wish that wasn't the case, I have to respect that. As far as the second reason, I'm only your client for another week, so I didn't think that applied."

"Oh, I get it," Mac said. "Since my fuck buddies contract seems so foreign to you, you must be one of those relationship types." She knew she was being a bit unreasonable, but she couldn't help it. Being around Alex seemed to short-circuit her brain.

His face grew serious. "Actually, I am. Which is why I'm disappointed that you won't consider going on a real date with me."

"I wasn't aware you'd asked me on a real date."

"You're right," he said, nodding his head. "Mac, would you do me the honor of accompanying me on a date this Thursday night?"

Wasn't he listening? She didn't do dates. *And, yet, you want to go on a real date with him so bad, you don't want to say no.* Mac briefly adverted her eyes from the intensity of his. She could either say yes and go on what she knew would be an amazing date with a great guy. Or, she could say no and always wonder what it would have been like to go on a normal date with a man who genuinely seemed interested in her as much as she was him.

"Okay," she said. "I'll go out on a date with you. But I'm not promising anything past that first date."

His eyes studied hers for a few seconds. "Deal," he said. When his lips curled to the side in a smile that was as equally sneaky as it was sexy, she knew she was in deep. Real deep.

CHAPTER 5

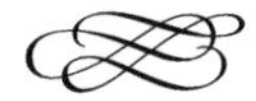

Alex glanced around the Boston steakhouse restaurant, spotting Mac at the table he'd personally requested. Although he'd only just asked her out a few days ago, he felt like he'd been waiting months to take her out.

"Hello, Mac," he said when he approached. "You look beautiful." She was wearing a midnight blue dress that fit her like a glove and her light brown curls were flowing around her shoulders. *What I'd give to run my fingers through that beautiful mass of hair.* Tonight wasn't about sex. It wasn't about work. It wasn't about Feng-Shui. It was about him and Mac getting to know each other on a deeper level, and if he were lucky, he'd be able to convince her to go on another date with him before this date ended.

"Thank you," she said with a smile. "You look nice, too."

"Thanks." He'd chosen to wear a pair of black slacks and a light-grey shirt. Judging by Mac's appreciative glance, he'd say she liked how he looked.

They glanced over the menu and placed their drink and food order when their waitress arrived.

"Did you get here okay?" he asked after they'd ordered.

"Oh, yeah," she said. "I've been here a couple times with my mom."

"It's just you and your sister, McKenna, right? The one who you were with at Owen and Ava's wedding?"

"Yes, just the two of us," Mac said with a smile. "She's two years younger than me, but she acts like she's two years older."

"I know the feeling," Alex said with a laugh. "Shane is three years younger than me, but growing up, he always tried to act like my big brother. Up until our parents passed away, he was a pain in my side."

"Oh no," Mac said. "I didn't know your parents passed away. How old were you?"

"I was twenty-one and Shane was eighteen."

"What happened?"

Alex clenched his jaw, still finding the topic difficult to discuss despite the time that had passed. "My dad was a marine, so we moved around a lot, but I was mainly raised in Texas. Shane and I were away at college when two men broke into my parents' home and robbed them. My parents had waited to have kids until they were almost forty, so my dad had just entered early retirement the year before. Typically, they weren't home on a Saturday night since they were really involved with the community, but that night, they'd stayed home because my dad wasn't feeling well. Them being home surprised the robbers who we later found out had hit up three other empty homes in the neighborhood that night.

"My parents surprised them by being home. From what the police told us, they assume my dad swung a bat at one and the other snuck up and shot him. My mom probably ran to my dad and they shot her, too."

The waiter delivered their drinks. "Oh my gosh," Mac said, clenching her chest. She reached over the table and placed her hand in his. "I'm so sorry you and your brother had to go through something so horrific."

Alex gently squeezed her hand before he took a sip of his Cognac. "Nothing had ever happened like that in our community. It's still hard to deal with, but Shane and I were lucky to have each other. I graduated a few months later, and although Shane was going to school in Texas, neither one of us wanted to move back to our hometown despite the fact that we had some other family in the state. I'd gone to school for environmental engineering and my dad's friend had an environmental engineer firm here in Boston and offered me a job. I accepted, and a couple months later, I'd moved here and Shane had transferred to a university nearby."

"Do you ever go back to visit your hometown?" Mac asked, before sipping her drink.

"Nah, I haven't been able to go back since it happened."

"I don't blame you," she said. "My grandmother, Pearl, was from Texas and since our mom was always moving us around, we found comfort in visiting my grandmother. I have a couple aunts, uncles, and cousins in the state, but my grandmother passed away three years ago and I haven't been to Texas since."

"Do you get grief from your other family members for not visiting?" he asked.

"I do," she said. "In my case, my family all lost the matriarch, so they don't understand why my sister and I won't visit. I know my grandmother was close to all her grandchildren, but since most of them still lived in the state, they got to see her all the time. For McKenna and me, we rarely got to see her despite the fact that we talked to her all the time. So her death hit me hard. In fact, I'm still not completely healed."

"I don't think you ever completely heal," he said. "When someone close to you passes away, the most we can hope for is to find a way to cope with the death and move on with life the way we know they would have wanted us to. For years, Shane and I were mad at the world. Every time I went to visit a high school or college friend, all I could think about was the fact that their parents were still living, but I'd lost mine. It wasn't fair. Nothing felt fair. And for me, getting that job at the firm was my life saver. I'm sure Shane felt the same way when the company recruited him."

"Is it the same firm you both work at now?"

"Yeah, it is."

Her eyes lit up. "That's amazing. So you're now CEO of the firm that in some ways, saved your life from a bought of depression."

"Sure did." He smiled as he thought about how much better his life got once he started living life instead of being angry at it. "That's probably why I take my job so seriously. Pat wasn't only my mentor and my dad's best friend, he took Shane and I under his wing when we needed guidance and stability. I owe that man everything, so I refuse to let his legacy die. The only problem is the fact that two employees who were in leadership roles left the company two years ago and took some of our top clients with them. They even secretly recruited one of my top assistant project managers recently."

"That's shady," Mac said as their food arrived. "But you can't let them win. When I first opened my consulting business, I got a mean side-eye from every interior decorator within a fifty-mile radius. Not only did they not understand my business, but a few major interior designers lost big clients to me, so in exchange, they tried to taint my name in the industry for a few years."

Alex shook his head. "People will stop at nothing to get ahead. And what's truly sad about it is that at the end of the day, sometimes the bad guys do win. When that happens, it's hard to have faith in humanity."

"I question humanity every day," Mac said with a laugh. "So, for me, stupid people will get a stupid reaction. I know better than to fight fire with fire, so I fight fire with water instead. In the words of one of my idols, Michelle Obama, when they go low, we go high."

"Cheers to that," Alex said, raising his glass in a toast. "And if they go lower?"

Mac squinted her eyes in thought. "Maybe we rise even higher?"

He nodded his head. "I like that."

"Thanks," she said with a smile. For the next few minutes, they ate in silence. Alex loved how easy Mac was to talk to, especially when she let her guard down. He'd already known that fact to be true based off the first time they'd met, but every time they talked, he was even more surprised by the things they had in common.

"I meant to ask," she said after she took another bite of her food. "In companies like yours, doesn't the management usually have to sign a non-compete clause?"

"Yeah, we do, but it's not for that long," he said. "Pat never wanted to make his people sign a non-compete contract for more than two years, and many—myself included—always thought it was way too lenient for a smaller firm. However, that's Pat for you. Always believing that people are better than they are. The entire staff loved him, and when I took over as CEO two years ago, it wasn't a complete shock because everyone knew I was being groomed to take over. However, not everyone liked it when I officially stepped into the role."

Mac shook her head. "Let me guess. Two members of the leadership team quit out of jealously?"

"That was partially it." Alex took another sip of his Cognac to erase the bitter taste he still had in his mouth when he spoke about this topic. "One of the employees who left was Kimberly, my serious girlfriend at the time."

Mac's eyes widened. "She really left when you were named CEO instead of staying and supporting you?"

"Yes, and that wasn't even the worst part."

"How could that not be the worst part?" Mac asked. "Unless she was cheating on you with the other person who left the company?"

"Actually," he said. "That's right. She was having an affair with the other person who quit the company the day I was named CEO."

Mac's hand flew to her mouth. "Wow. I can't imagine you having to work with your ex and the man she cheated on you with. I think you're better off that they left."

"*Woman,*" Alex said. "Kimberly was cheating on me with Samantha, another woman, not a man." He finished off his Cognac. "Did I mention that I'd dated Samantha when I'd first started working at the firm? We started the same month."

Alex waved over the waitress and ordered another drink. It was only after he'd ordered that he noticed Mac was still looking at him with her eyes wide open.

* * *

"DAMN," she said for the third time. She was really trying to find a more eloquent word to repeat, but she couldn't think of one.

"It sounds more fucked up than it really is," Alex said. "Was I hurt by the betrayal of my current girlfriend and an ex who I still considered a friend at the time? Yes. But the more I thought about Kimberly, the more I realized that we wouldn't have worked anyway. After they quit, I had a long talk with Kim and I realized that although she was wrong, she was right about the fact that I never loved her the way that I should have. We never really had anything in common besides work. I may have even proposed because we'd been together for four years and I felt like that's what we should do, but it wasn't what was best for us. In some strange way, I'm glad they found each other and I'm happy for them in that sense. However, the fact that they have teamed up with our rival company and are now going after some of our biggest clients is what I'm having the most difficulty with."

Mac looked at him with a newfound appreciation. "Yeah, that's frustrating, but what they have that you don't is your firm's legacy that Pat built. They may have worked at your firm for a while and built relationships with clients, but you're impressive, Alex, and I know you can win back those accounts."

He smiled in a bashful way she hadn't seen before. "Thanks for the vote of confidence. I've actually gotten back three of the five so far. I'm sure they'll try and convert others, or even target more of my staff, but you're right. Reminding our clients that they are appreciated and thanking them for supporting Pat's firm for all these years is a good way to start."

"It is," she said. "And I admire you for not letting the situation with your ex-girlfriend and friend affect you. I think I would have been too pissed to think rationally or be happy for them."

"Well," Alex said as he titled his head. "According to Shane and Pete, I did do something drastic."

"What did you do?" she asked before she took another sip of her White Russian.

"I took a vow of celibacy the day I became CEO when I decided that having meaningless sex was pointless if I couldn't make love to a woman I cared about."

And cue White Russian all over the white tablecloth. "I'm so sorry," Mac said as she took her napkin and wiped Alex's arm.

"It's okay," he said with a laugh. "Your reaction is warranted."

"I'm just… I can't…" *Gather your thoughts, Mac.* "But why?"

"I think I was just fed up at the time," Alex said. "I felt excited because I was CEO, but I also felt hurt. Betrayed. Confused. Don't get me wrong, almost everyone at the company was happy for me and I have an amazing staff. But I just felt empty after the Kimberly situation."

"I understand," she said. "Or at least, I'm trying to understand."

"I appreciate your honesty," Alex said with a smile. "I guess in order to explain, you need to know where I stand on relationships." He looked at her with that intensity she was getting used to. "Most men like playing the field and, yes, there was a time in my life when I was playing the field and bedding women whose name I couldn't even remember. At the time, I thought I was living the life. I didn't care about serious girlfriends or monogamous relationships. And then my parents died, and my entire world turned upside down. I may have legally been an adult when they passed, but I was still a kid in so many ways. I remember being in the middle of having sex with one of my frequent ladies at the time and I realized that I wasn't into it. And it wasn't because the sex wasn't good. It was because so many parts of my life didn't have meaning without my parents being around, including sex.

"My parents had a beautiful marriage, and no matter how many fights they got into, I knew they loved one another. I remember going to sleep that night with a new goal in mind—to try and have more meaningful relationships in life. And I'm not just talking about relationships with women I dated. I'm talking relationships with my brother, with my friends, and my college buddies like Owen. With family who, even though I didn't want to go to Texas, I could have them visit me in Boston, so I reached out."

"So, no one-night stands?" she asked. "No flings? Only relationships?"

"I still have a few flings and one-night stands," he said with a laugh. "I didn't just give up everything all at once. I eased into it and it took years. But the reason being celibate when I was named CEO was easy for me was because at thirty-two, I realized I wanted more. I deserved more. So I put all my energy into my career."

Mac had so many questions she didn't even know where to start. "Are you waiting for marriage?"

"Was I waiting for marriage? I hadn't decided," he said with a shrug. "And then I met you..."

Her breathing stopped. "I messed up your celibacy plans?" she asked. "You broke your commitment to yourself because of me? Why would you do that?"

"Listen," Alex said as he reached over and took her hands in his. "I'm a grown ass man. I made the vow of celibacy because I didn't want to have meaningless sex. All you promised me when we met was a night of unrestrained bliss and that's exactly what I broke my vow for. A chance not to think. Not to stress. A night with a beautiful woman whose mouth, mind, and body had me hypnotized within the first couple minutes of conversation."

Swoon. She straightened in her chair, but kept her hands in his.

"Mac, the night I shared with you wasn't the night that I broke my commitment to myself. The night I shared with you was the night I finally experienced why I'd made the commitment in the first place. Nothing about what we shared was meaningless. Granted, we hadn't really known each other before that night and I know you don't want anything serious, but even if we never have another night like the one we shared, it will always be a time I cherish. A time I remember as the night I knew that there was at least one women in this world who'd appreciate what I had to offer. It wasn't just sex for me that night and now that I know you more, I think it's safe to say that the night we shared was more than just sex for you, too."

He ran his thumbs in small circles on her hands. "I'm not trying to send you running in the opposite direction, but my dad always told me that when you've met your special match, you'll know. You'll know it in the way you talk to each other. In the way you make love with each other. You'll feel it in your bones. In your heart." She didn't think it was possible, but his eyes got even more intense. "When you've found your match, the timing may not be perfect, but when you're finally on the same page, you won't be able to keep your hands off each other."

Mac let out a breath she'd been unaware she was holding. As she stared back at a man who she was growing closer to with each passing day, she couldn't help but wonder if she'd finally met someone who wouldn't break her heart. The idea scared her more than she cared to admit, but she had to face the facts. Men like

Alex didn't grow on trees. They were bred from birth as one of the few leaders in a pack of wolves.

Alexander Carter was a *real* man and every time he looked at her, spoke to her, smiled at her, openly shared a part of himself with her without asking anything in return, a piece of her heart fell for him. Hard. Fast. Unexpected.

Be careful, Mac, the devil on her shoulder whispered. *Your time with Alex is only temporary. You aren't built for forever. He could never be yours.*

Typically, Mac was all too willing to listen to that negative voice whispering in her ear, but not tonight. Tonight, she was soaking in everything that Alexander Carter represented no matter how nervous it made her. Tonight, she would allow herself to believe that she truly was his perfect match. She would place her inhibitions on mute and enjoy what was easily the best date she'd ever had.

"Your place or mine?" she asked, holding his gaze.

His lips curled to the side in a knowing smirk. "How about yours this time."

CHAPTER 6

Alex took his keys out of the ignition and tried not to smile too hard, but he couldn't help it. He was in a damn good mood as he followed Mac to her condo and it wasn't just because he was being blessed with the opportunity to spend another night with her. He was also confident that based off how well dinner had gone, he predicted greater conversations in the near future.

Tonight, he'd taken a huge risk by laying his cards out on the table for Mac to either pick up the deck, shuffle and play a game, or place the cards back in the card box. To his surprise, she'd chosen to shuffle the cards and he was damn glad she'd made that choice.

"Come on in," she said after she'd unlocked the door.

"I like your place," he said as he stepped into the open floor of the main area. "Now that I'm learning all about Feng-Shui, I can see how you've incorporated harmony into your home." He looked at the yellow tulips on the table, blue striped rug in the living room, and bright red dish on the dining room table. Her style was definitely more eclectic than his, but it worked. "The colors and patterns seem to really work well together."

Mac walked over to where he was sitting at the kitchen island and handed him a glass of wine. "I'll make a believer out of you yet."

"I'm already a believer," he said. "You've managed to change a group of engineers into believers, too by adding certain elements to our conference rooms that we never considered before. I was pleasantly surprised yesterday to walk into the office and see the boring rectangular tables and basic chairs replaced by a cream curved table, blue chairs with elongated backs, green succulents at every table, and abstract art of the walls. Everyone loves the changes, and maybe it's just my imagination, but they seem happier to schedule meetings now."

"That's just the harmony working," she said as she took a sip of her wine. He watched the way her tongue peeked out to catch a drop that was sliding down the glass.

Alex felt his pants grow tighter in the crotch area. *Shit.* Although they both knew how the night would end, he wasn't trying to rush her into anything. They should at least be able to share a glass of wine without him thinking about ripping her clothes off.

"What's one of your biggest fears when it comes to love?" she asked.

Alex took a sip of his wine and settled into the stool. "I've always worried that I'd fall for a woman who wouldn't love me back," he said. "She'd get to know me and decide that I wasn't worth her love."

Mac shook her head. "I don't think that would ever happen," she said. "Maybe I'm too far gone in my Alex-induced lust fog to think clearly, but I can't imagine any woman ever thinking that you are unworthy of her love."

Alex quirked an eyebrow. "Alex-induced lust fog?"

She playfully slapped his arm. "You're such a man. Is that the only thing you heard?"

"No, but it definitely stood out." He laughed. "But thank you for saying that. What about you? What's one of your fears when it comes to falling in love?"

Mac sighed as she placed her wine glass on the island. "I have plenty," she finally said. "But the biggest one is probably that I will fall in love with a man and he'll fall in love with me back. Then, maybe months or years later, once we're past the infatuation phase, he'll decide that he doesn't want me anymore."

Alex gently rubbed her cheek with the back of his hand. "I don't think you have to worry about that happening. You have so many amazing qualities and any man who doesn't recognize that you're the type of woman he can be with for the rest of his life isn't worth your time."

"Thank you, but that's not all," she said, leaning against his hand. "The reason I prefer frivolous relationships is not because I fear commitment. It's because I fear that I won't be able to recognize a relationship that was doomed from the start. To most, there isn't a difference, but there's a distinct difference to me."

She reached for her wine and took another sip before she continued. "My mom is about to marry her *sixth* husband. My dad was her first, but when McKenna and I were younger, my dad got into some trouble with the law by counterfeiting credit cards. So, our mom was the main provider. I've always had a close relationship with both of my parents, but they didn't get along much. My mom resented my dad for getting in trouble with the law and my dad thought she loved him enough to wait for him to get his act together. One day, my dad picked up McKenna and I from school and said our mom no longer loved him and he had to leave. Suddenly, we were only seeing my dad on weekends and it was obvious that losing my mother broke his heart."

"Do you resent your mom for divorcing your dad?"

Mac sighed. "I guess in a way, I did back then. Sometimes I wonder if I still do. After my parents divorced, we were constantly moving to wherever my mom's husband at the time wanted us to live. Husbands number two and three weren't that memorable. They both left, one claiming that he could no longer be with a woman with kids and the other saying he fell out of love with her. In a way, it was sad to watch my mom deal with husband number three since the reason he gave her was the exact same reason she'd divorced my father. Number three also hadn't known my mom was pregnant at the time and she miscarried from the stress of losing him."

"Damn, I'm sorry, Mac," he said. "What about the last two?"

"Number four and five were more civil, but regardless, they all left in some way, shape, or form. During that time, my dad was on his second wife, but that ended for reasons I still don't know. Now, he's on wife number three and he seems happy… For now."

"You don't think it will last?"

Mac shook her head. "It's not that I think it won't last, but my parents seem to get married faster than a presidential term. I've had more step-parents than I have had presidents. I love my mom and dad with all my heart, but I don't think I ever realized that I'd developed quite a few relationship fears based off what I watched them go through. For my dad, it was hard to watch him lose my mom. And for my mom, it was difficult to see her heart crumble each and every time, so by the time I was able to date, I'd already formed some pretty bad perceptions."

"I can understand that," he said, dropping one hand to her knee. "You based love off of what you saw. The fact that your mother stopped loving your dad, and some of your mom's exes eventually stopped loving her meant you didn't want the same thing to happen to you, so why even fall in love?"

"I fell in love once," Mac said. "His name was Prince and I dated him through most of college and some time after. There's not much that I would thank him for, but if I had to pick one thing, I guess it would be that he did show me that I am capable of giving my love to someone."

Of course, you are, he thought. "Why did you guys break up?"

"Well, that's the fun part," she said with a smile that didn't reach her eyes. "Before we'd graduated college, Prince and I had purchased a place in his Atlanta hometown. His idea, not mine. His credit was bad, so I had no problem putting the small home in my name. I moved there as planned after we graduated, and at the same time my mom had decided to move with husband number four to Boston. We were happy…for about two months. I'd uprooted my entire life, gotten a job at an interior design firm, only to come home one day and find a note on the refrigerator saying that he couldn't be in a serious relationship anymore and had to leave. He'd gone to live with his high school girlfriend who he dated before we met. To top it off, he'd moved out all of *our* furniture and had only left the mattress and my personal belongings."

"Shit," Alex said. "That had to have been hard for you. What did you do?"

"I did what I had to do," she said. "First, I tracked his ass down, cursed him out, and keyed his 1976 Mercedes that he loved so much."

"Not the car." Alex clenched his chest.

"I had to hit him where it hurt. After that, I picked myself up, gathered all of my stuff, and drove to Boston since my mom was there. I still own the house in Atlanta, so I rent it out and have a nice family that has lived there for the past six years. But Boston is my home now."

"You're a strong woman," Alex said with a smile. "And although I hate that you had to go through that, I'm glad that you're in Boston now. All the obstacles you've had to overcome are what made you who you are today."

"What?" she asked with a laugh. "Pissed-off and hesitant to love?"

"No." He brushed one fallen curl from her face and stuck it behind her ear. "Strong and resilient with a heart that knows the type of love she deserves and won't settle for anything less."

Her eyes softened and he fell for her even more. He didn't

need to take one of those online quizzes to know what was in his heart. He was falling in love with her. He wasn't surprised by his feelings at all and he'd seen them coming a mile away.

Mac leaned toward him, her curls falling over her shoulders as she did. She searched his eyes, looking for something that he hoped she found. He wasn't ready to express his love—mainly because he wasn't sure if she was ready to hear it—but he did want to be as transparent as possible.

"In case you're wondering," he said. "When I think about giving my heart to someone, you're the woman who comes to mind and have for months."

She squinted in confusion. "But you barely knew me a few months ago."

"I'd had a night with you." He searched her eyes in return. "An amazing, life-changing night. That was all I needed to know what type of woman you are."

She laughed nervously. "Some men spend years with a woman and still aren't sure if she's his future, yet you—"

"And I," he said cutting her off. "I spend one night with a woman and know that she's it for me."

Her eyes widened. *Good job, Alex. So much for not laying it on strong.*

"If we're being honest," she said in a low voice. "I guess what I was trying to say all night is that I truly do want to commit to someone, give my heart to the right person. I want someone to love me so much, that they can't imagine being with anyone else. I want to experience the type of love that consumes me, mind, body and soul."

"I can give that to you," he whispered. "If you let me."

The next move happened so fast, Alex wasn't sure who reached for whom first. Their lips met in a heated kiss as he lifted her from her stool.

"Bedroom?"

"That way." Alex walked in the direction that Mac had pointed her finger, careful not to run into anything along the way. Once they reached her bed, he gently laid her down in the center, only breaking the kiss to remove their clothes.

"The chemistry we have is crazy," Mac said as clothes were quickly discarded.

Alex smiled down at her naked body. "It's the best kind of crazy." He was already anxious to get his hands on that ass he'd been fantasizing about for weeks.

Alex kissed her feet, lightly sucking each toe before planting kisses up her body. When he reached her breasts, he flicked his tongue over her nipples, enjoying the way they hardened before his eyes. Mac kissed his forearms and chest, opening her legs wider so that he could fit in between them.

For them to have been so frantic moments before, now felt different. Once he reached her face, he kissed each cheek before gazing into her eyes. Tonight, they'd done a lot of talking, and although Alex was glad they'd learned so much about each other, he welcomed the silence that enveloped them while they explored one another.

Leaning up on his forearms, he protected them both and slid past her folds, positioning himself in front of her opening. Her eyes were closed in anticipation, but Alex wanted her to see his face when he entered her, so he waited for her to open them.

The extra seconds it took for her to open her eyes gave him the chance to admire her even more. *She's mine,* he thought as a smile crept across her face. Alex couldn't help the feelings coursing through his body. He felt like she was perfect for him in so many ways, and in turn, he was willing to give her all of him. *Hell, she practically already has all of me.* It was safe to say he'd do just about anything to make the smile she was giving him a permanent one.

Slowly, her eyes flickered open. He'd barely seen her full pupils before he thrust into her core, relishing in the dreamy combination of appreciation and enjoyment reflected in her eyes.

"Alex," she said breathlessly. "Oh God."

He moved in slow, silky strokes, wanting to touch a part of her that she often kept guarded. It didn't take long before she was meeting his strokes, her hips coming off the bed and joining with his in perfect unison. They made love as if they'd danced this dance a thousand times before, and in more ways than one, Alex felt like that was true.

He'd waited his entire life to meet a woman like Mac and just when he'd given up hope on finding her, she'd approached him at a friend's wedding, changing his life forever. He was even more grateful that his employees had purchased her consulting services as a gift. He didn't even want to think about what his future would look like without her in it.

"Flip us over," she whispered. Alex switched their positions so that she was on top. The minute she moved her hips forward, he threw his head back on the pillow. It didn't take long for them to get into another good rhythm, each buck of her hips implanting Alex deeper into her core. The fact that his hands were filled with her plump ass cheeks was an added bonus.

Mac leaned forward. "I'm close," she breathed into his ear.

"Me, too." He'd been close before they'd switched positions, so he was hanging on by a thread now. Seconds later, Mac exploded in a wave of pure ecstasy, moaning into the ceiling in a way he hadn't heard before. The sexy purr of her voice and increase of movements sent him over the edge right with her in a groan that he was sure sounded anything but sexy.

"Wow," Mac said as she fell to his chest.

"I concur." Mentally, physically and emotionally, making love with Mac had been everything he'd remembered and more. After a few minutes, Mac stood from the bed.

"Get comfortable, I'll be right back." She slipped out of the bedroom.

Alex quickly discarded the protection in her bathroom, then returned to the bedroom to follow her instructions. He positioned himself in the middle of the bed, his erection jumping in anticipation of what Mac was up to. She was gone for a few minutes, but when she returned, he noticed she'd remained completely naked, except for her black pumps.

"Damn, you look sexy as hell." He leaned forward to get out of bed.

"Not so fast, Mr. Carter," she said, sashaying across the room. "We had dinner earlier, but we left before dessert and I *love* dessert." He noticed she had some whip cream and chocolate syrup in her hand.

"I thought we just had dessert," he said, referring to their lovemaking.

"That was the cherry on top," she said. "We skipped the ice cream sundae." She placed the whip cream on the nightstand. "Let's start with the chocolate syrup."

Alex wasn't sure where he'd expected her to squirt the syrup, but he was pretty sure his erection wasn't what he'd thought. However, as her mouth enclosed around the shaft of his penis and her tongue rolled up and down in languid caresses to remove the chocolate syrup, he realized thinking was no longer on the menu. All he could do was embrace the pleasure that Mac's mouth elicited within him.

When she added the whip cream to her tasty dick sundae, he wasn't able to hold back the second orgasm that was trying to escape.

"Mac, I'm close," he warned. He waited for her to release him from her mouth, but instead, she increased the pressure of her licks, sucking him deeper until he hit the back of her throat.

"Mac," he said again, but it was no use. Grabbing the back of her head, he pumped into her warm mouth, already jumping back on the ecstasy train, and this time, the train appeared to be coming at full speed ahead.

"Fuckkkkk." He drawled the explicative as he came in an orgasm more powerful than any he'd ever experienced orally. If

Mac had had any hesitation about the way he'd gripped her head while she sucked his dick, she hadn't let on. *Based off that big smile on her face, I'd say she rather liked it.*

After Mac took a wet towel to clean up the sundae, Alex pulled her to him for round two, but apparently, she was already two steps ahead of him. She protected them this time and eased him into her core, her vaginal muscles clenching around his length. As they lay there, unmoving and experiencing the physical intimacy of their relationship, Alex had one thought and one thought only. *You have to tell her as soon as possible. You're falling in love this woman and she deserves to know exactly how you feel.*

CHAPTER 7

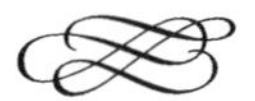

The morning light seeping through the blinds in the bedroom woke him up. He reached for Mac only to find her side of the bed empty. He got out of bed and walked out the bedroom to check the other rooms. After doing a thorough search and not finding her there, he went back to the bedroom and spotted a piece of paper on her nightstand that he hadn't seen before.

A kiss... He already had one piece of paper with her lip prints on it, but apparently, she thought he needed another one. *At least she left a note this time.* He flipped over the piece of paper.

Alex, thank you for last night. It was
amazing. I have an event to attend
today and needed some time
to think. Just lock the door on your
way out. I'll call you when I'm ready.

xoxo Mac

DAMN. Alex laid back on her bed and ran his fingers down his face. Did he wish Mac was still there? Of course. Did he regret anything that happened between them last night? Absolutely not. Was he annoyed that she apparently had on her running shoes again? *Hell* yeah. He knew she was a runner, but she'd left him in her own home. Her home, not his. That was a new one. He'd give her time to think since things had moved pretty fast, but he wanted to find her and make sure she was okay.

He glanced at the ceiling. "After I find my woman, I'm hiding all her gym shoes." Unfortunately, he had something important to take care of first. But after that, he was finding Mac and talking this through.

After he finished getting dressed, he glanced at the floor of her closet taking note of her heels and sandals on the floor. Had he found a pair of gym shoes or two, he couldn't promise that he wouldn't have confiscated them.

* * *

"PULL YOURSELF TOGETHER, MAC." She'd been chanting those same four words for hours, yet, she still wasn't any closer to having her shit together as she was before she'd left her condo.

Last night with Alex had been amazing. Even better than amazing. It had been exhilarating. Enlightening. Exciting. Electrifying. *Calm it down with the 'E' words Mac.* She wasn't even sure there was a word out there for how she'd felt last night, but if there was, that was the word she would use.

When she'd awakened in the wee hours of the morning, she'd expected that same excitement to continue, but instead, all of her positive feelings had been replaced with panic and the realization that she wasn't just enjoying her time with Alexander Carter. She was falling in love with him.

Sometime during the course of the Let's-Get-Naked-For-A-Wild-Night when they'd first met and Let's-Open-Up-About-All-

Our-Insecurities-And-Overcome-Them-Together that they'd recently had, Mac had managed to begin to fall hopelessly in love with the one man she knew she should have avoided. She knew he had the ability to steal her heart. He was gorgeous, smart, successful. Too damn charming for his own good. *And don't forget Daisy, the cutest cat ever. Seriously, who can avoid a man with a pet?* Mac shook the thoughts from her head.

"I'm losing my mind," she said as she walked into the building and looked for her sister. After a quick search, she spotted her near a closed-door room.

"I was worried you were going to be late," McKenna said. "But I'm glad you're here. You are not going to like what I have to tell you."

"If it's bad news, can it wait?" Mac asked. "I've had such a long night, but today isn't about me and I don't want us to lose sight of what's important."

"I know, sis," McKenna said. "I can see the stress written on your face. But I wouldn't say anything if it wasn't extremely important. But when I tell you, please try and keep an open mind."

"Did something happen to Mom?" Mac asked in a worried tone.

"Well, no."

"Is anyone else in the family sick? Is it Quinn, Raven, Ryleigh or Ava?"

"No," McKenna said. "No one is sick or dying."

"Then what is it?" Mac glanced at the time on her cell phone. "Because we're supposed to be in this room in exactly one minute."

"Ugh, you're impossible," McKenna said. "Let's just head in. We'll talk later."

"Okay," Mac said as she pushed open the doors. The moment she stepped into the room, she froze, her eyes venturing to the only person who always captured her complete attention.

"Alex!" she exclaimed. "What are you doing here?"

Alex walked over to her with the sexiest smile on his face. "Hello, Julia Roberts."

Mac frowned. "Why the Julia reference?"

He glanced down at her feet and for the first time since she'd left the house that morning did she notice that she'd paired her lilac dress with her purple and teal gym shoes. *Crap, I didn't even remember to grab my heels.*

"You're like Julia Roberts in *Runaway Bride*," Alex said. "Except sexier and apparently a little easier to track down."

It was then that she saw her mom and Rick patiently watching the exchange. Shane was also there and gave a slight wave when her eyes landed on him.

"I don't understand," she said. "You contacted my sister to ask her where I'd be today?"

"Nope," McKenna said from behind her. "I had nothing to do with this. And apparently, none of us did."

"What?" Mac asked. "I'm confused."

"I only got here five minutes before you did," Alex said. "But from what I pieced together in that short amount of time is that Patrick Marx – who just so happens to be the former CEO of my engineer firm and my dad's best friend – is none other than your mom's new fiancé and soon-to-be husband."

Mac's eyes flew to her mom and Rick. "Really? I thought your name was Rick."

Rick, also known as Pat and Patrick, shrugged. "I was known as Pat or Patrick in the engineer world and when I retired and met your mother, I wanted to enjoy my retirement and decided to start going by the name my friends used to call me back in college. Rick, short for Patrick.

"Sis, as much as I know you and Alex obviously need to talk, Mom and Rick have to get married and city hall doesn't play games when it comes to waiting."

"Right," Mac said. "Let's do this." She'd ask Alex to expand on his Julia Roberts reference after.

* * *

She's so adorable. Sitting across from him in the after-wedding lunch at a nearby restaurant in another dress that made his mouth water with a pair of gym shoes that served as a subtle reminder of why he still needed to hide hers, he didn't think he'd ever seen a woman more beautiful.

When he'd walked into the venue and spotted McKenna, he was immediately confused. Then when Pat introduced McKenna, who he'd already known, and Marlene, it didn't take long for Alex to piece everything together despite the fact that Shane had been laughing hard at his expense.

Knowing that Mac's mother and his father-figure had just tied the knot only motivated him more to tell Mac how he felt. He'd never seen Pat as happy as he was now, and the fact that he'd finally found that once-in-a-lifetime love that he'd always craved in Marlene served as a reminder that it didn't matter how long or short you've known someone. Whatever's meant to be will be, but when love knocked on your door, you'd better answer.

"I'd like to make a toast," Pat said as he clamped his glass.

"You want to make a toast on your own wedding day?" Alex teased.

"I sure do." He glanced down at Marlene. "If you would have told me a few years ago that I'd find a woman who meant more to me than life itself, I would have placed a bet against it. I've spent more than half my life searching for the type of love I watched others find and had been unsuccessful. Imagine my surprise when I found you. A woman who'd been through her share of heartache only to come out from the other side on top. Marlene, your beauty shines inside and out, and you're one of the most selfless women I've ever met. Today, you have made me the happiest man in the world. Here's to the rest of our lives together."

Alex couldn't help but observe Mac after a speech like that.

Alex may have been thirty-five years younger than Pat, but he'd waited most of his life for a woman like Mac.

"I'm going to bring up the elephant in the room," McKenna said as she turned her attention to Alex and Mac. "Alex, are you helping Mac with the pact? Inquiring minds want to know."

"And by inquiring minds, she means all of us," Shane said. "The four of us had a chance to talk before you two arrived."

Alex looked at the group. "What pact?"

Mac turned to McKenna. "McKenna, you told everyone about the pact? Seriously?"

McKenna shrugged. "Sorry, it just kind of slipped out. I didn't say much. Only that you and your friends all agreed to get married soon and that you hated losing bets and wanted to be the first to get married."

Alex laughed when Mac did a face palm. "You and your friends made a pact to get married?"

Mac's eyes reluctantly met his. "Yes, it was a stupid pact that I didn't even want to participate in, but like McKenna said, I hate losing."

"How long was the timeline?"

Mac hesitated and glanced around the table. "We're all family now," Pat said. "Might as well clue us in."

Mac sighed. "We have a year to get married. The deadline is in less than ten months."

"Did you make the pact at Owen and Ava's wedding?"

Mac squinted. "How did you guess that?"

"You said you had a year and less than ten months are left. They married almost three months ago, when you and I met."

"Was he the young man you were telling me about?" Marlene asked McKenna. "The best man who Mackenzie couldn't keep her eyes off of?"

Mac glanced from her mom to her sister. "Sis, please tell me that you didn't tell mom about Alex."

McKenna shrugged. "Okay, then I won't tell you."

Alex would have laughed at Mac giving her sister the death stare, if he hadn't been so focused on Shane's sneaky smile. *I know that look. What is he up to?*

"Since you hate to lose," Shane said to Mac. "You should just marry my brother and put him out of his misery."

Mac shook her head. "As much as I like your brother, I would never do that to him. I've already decided on another route." She cringed and Alex assumed she hadn't meant to say the last part.

"Another route?" He asked. "As in, you plan on losing the bet?"

"Ha!" McKenna said. "Mac doesn't lose. I think she meant to say that she already has another plan to find a husband."

Alex's eyes flew to Mac's. "You've been dating someone else while we've been dating?"

Marlene perked up in her seat. "Alex, you and my daughter are dating? Oh, that's wonderful news. Isn't it Rick?"

"Great news." He raised a glass to Alex.

"Wait, what?" Mac raised her hands in the air. "Can everyone stop making assumptions. One, Alex and I went on a date and yes, we met at the wedding, but we're still figuring it out. Two, no I haven't been seeing anyone else. And lastly, McKenna is right. I don't like to lose, but I'm not sharing my plans with anyone, so can we just forget about the pact?"

Not likely. Eventually, the table started talking about possible places for Marlene and Pat to take their honeymoon instead of focusing on Alex and Mac. Even so, Alex still couldn't shake the eerie feeling that he wasn't going to like whatever plan she had for the pact.

"I know you said you need space," Alex whispered to Mac so that only she could hear. "But I think we need to talk about a few things, so just let me know when you're ready."

Mac glanced at him. "I agree, and I'm sorry for walking out this morning. We definitely should talk."

"Great, how about dinner tomorrow night?"

Mac laughed. "You don't waste any time, do you?"

Alex smiled. "I'm a patient guy... sometimes."

"Well, Mr. Patient Guy, I would love to meet tomorrow night, but I have a meeting with a new client. But I planned on stopping by your office with my team the next day before another meeting that I have. Want to find some time to talk then?"

"No, I think we should meet three nights from now then. I know you have a lot to do at the office and I don't want to take time away from that."

"Okay," Mac said in a soft voice. "Sounds like a plan." They sat there staring at one another for a few seconds, neither saying anything.

In all honesty, there was so much Alex wanted to say, he didn't know where to start. He was glad he'd have a couple days to gather his thoughts and think of the best way to handle his relationship with Mac. She may be unsure of her feelings for him, but the one thing he was certain of was that there was no way Mac was going to marry someone else to fulfill a pact.

CHAPTER 8

Okay, girl. You got this. Mac had been chanting those words since she left her office. Tonight, she was meeting with Dennis Collier, one of her newest clients who she was briefly involved with five years ago.

She'd originally met Dennis when a kid on a skateboard had knocked into her on a busy downtown Boston street. In the mist of her trying not to fall on her butt, she spilled her coffee down her blouse and the contents in her purse on the ground.

She'd been running late for a client meeting and nothing had been going right with her morning. As she struggled to retrieve the fallen items from her purse before people stomped over them, Dennis had appeared and helped her. After a few dates, both had realized they were too much alike to date and agreed that it was best that they remain friends.

Mac found a spot three blocks from her destination and exited her car. "Damn, it's cold." She shivered as the chilly breeze wafted through her curls. Although she was used to east coast weather by now, Mac never understood how drastically the temperature seemed to drop in December. *What I would give for a cup of hot chocolate right now.* She didn't finish the thought because she knew it would be consumed with Alex. Lately, it seemed he was never far from her mind. Even when she thought of hot chocolate, coffee, or anything else to quench her thirst.

Mac still couldn't believe how crazy yesterday had been. What are the odds that the morning she realized her feelings for Alex were a lot deeper than anything she'd ever experienced was the same day she'd find out that she couldn't avoid him even if she tried.

Do I even still want to try? Granted, she'd told Alex she needed some space, but was space really what she wanted? *Of course space is what you want. You're about to marry another man!*

Well, technically it still wasn't solidified that she would marry Dennis, but based off the conversation she'd had with him a few days ago, he was prepared to sign the business marriage contract and even agreed to a divorce after a year. He'd also just moved his company to a new building and wanted Mac to Feng Shui his new office space.

As Mac rounded the corner and approached the restaurant she was meeting Dennis at, she pushed all thoughts of Alex aside. This meeting was an important one and she had to be focused. If everything went according to plan, Dennis would be the person to help her fulfill the pact she'd made with her friends.

Dennis was actually the first man to give her the idea of the business marriage contract for situations in which a spouse is needed to further a career. To some, the idea seemed absurd. However, to Mac and others who didn't believe in marriage for love, it was a necessity.

Are you sure you still don't believe in marriage for love? What about Alex? There it was again. That name she couldn't seem to forget. The man she wasn't even sure she wanted to forget.

"Ugh, this is so stupid," she groaned aloud, not caring if people passing by heard her. "Stay focused and stop thinking about him." She dropped her voice an octave lower when she caught a couple curious glances. "So what if he's sexy. And successful. And educated. And so good in bed it makes my toes curl." As she reached for the door of the restaurant, her thoughts carried back to the last time they'd had sex. For the life of her, she couldn't stop thinking about the intensity in his eyes when they made love. *Wait, made love?* Mac shook her head. *We have sex. We don't make love. What I do with Alex is purely physical. Don't forget that.* But even as the thought left her mind, she knew it wasn't completely true. Everything she did with Alex wasn't purely physical. From the very start, she'd discussed topics that Mac often kept private and in turn, Alex had been just as open.

When she was with Alex, she felt exposed. Unable to hide behind the mask she often wore. She was unable to put on the façade of only using men for sex because she'd opened up to Alex in ways she never thought she would. "Okay, so maybe the conversation is amazing. And he's sexy. So sexy." She gulped. "Extremely sexy."

"I believe you already said the word *sexy*." Mac jumped at the sound of the voice behind her. She didn't have to turn around to know who the voice belonged to.

"Alex," she said when she faced him. "What are you doing here?" He looked so good, she almost had to lift her jaw off the ground. Under the outside restaurant lighting, she could tell he was dressed in a charcoal business suit and white dress shirt, minus the tie. She couldn't stop her appreciative glance from observing ever part of him.

When her eyes returned to his, Alex smirked in a sexy way that turned her insides into a knot the size of Texas. "I'm meeting my brother Shane and a client for dinner. They are waiting for me inside." She blinked, having already forgotten that she'd asked him a question.

His eyes roamed up and down her body. She'd chosen to wear a sleek black dress and paired the dress with her favorite red Manalo pumps. Her curls were pulled atop her head in a high bun and her red velvet lipstick matched her heels.

"You look amazing," he said, hunger evident in his eyes. "Is the meeting you were telling me about yesterday at this restaurant too?"

"Yeah it is," she said, releasing the handle of the door. She couldn't even recall how long she'd been holding the door slightly open. "He's waiting for me inside."

"He?" Alex asked.

Mac's eyes widened. "Yeah, he. My client is a male." Their eyes held and Mac got the distinct impression that Alex wanted to ask her more, but didn't.

"I guess it's only fair for me to tell you that I've been walking behind you for a couple blocks. I called out to you once or twice, but you seemed lost in thought."

Crap! Had he heard me talking to myself. "Yeah, I was just doing some thinking."

"About us?" he asked.

"Um." She shuffled from one heel to the other. "Yes, I was."

Alex stepped closer to her and gently ran the back of his right hand down the side of her cheek. The move made her shiver, spreading warmth throughout her body. "Want to share any of those thoughts about us?" he asked.

"Share my thoughts..." Her voice was barely above a whisper.

"Yes," he said, placing a quick kiss on her lips. "What's going on in that beautiful brain of yours?"

"Um, my brain?" *What the hell! Use your words, Mac!*

Alex laughed. "If I had to guess, I'd say that you are starting to feel as strongly about me as I am you and you don't know how to handle your feelings. So let me help you work through them. What are you thinking?"

Mac swallowed. Hard. In all honesty, she was terrified to tell Alex that she was starting to fall in love with him. She was sure her eyes looked the size of saucers as she gazed up at the man who was slowly stealing her heart. As she often did when she needed to give herself some mental advice, she thought about words of Grandma Pearl.

Sweetie, a woman who chooses to be mute in a relationship will never be heard. If you don't speak up, you only have yourself to blame. And what you aren't willing to say to your man, another woman is more than willing to say.

Mac sighed. *I know Grandma Pearl. I know.*

"I guess I wanted to apologize to you again," Mac finally said. "I'm sorry for leaving you in my home before you woke up. I was just overwhelmed and confused."

Alex squinted. "Maybe I can help clear up any confusion."

Mac opened her mouth to respond, but the sound of a man clearing his throat behind Mac halted her answer.

"Hey Dennis," she said, realizing for the first time that he'd walked outside the restaurant. "So sorry I'm late."

"That's okay." Dennis looked from Mac to Alex. "I noticed you standing out here and wanted to make sure everything was okay."

"Everything is fine." Mac stepped back from Alex. Seeing Dennis was like throwing a bucket of cold water on her face and brought things back into perspective. "Alex, this is Dennis. My client. Dennis, this is Alex. My..." Her voice trailed off. *My what? Lover? Fuck buddy? Friend? Man I'm falling in love with?*

"I'm Mac's boyfriend," Alex said, before she had a chance to answer. It took a few seconds for Mac to register what Alex had said.

"Boyfriend?" Dennis asked. "Mac, is this some type of joke?"

"Uh."

"Why would it be a joke?" Alex asked.

"Well," Dennis said. "Tonight, Mac and I were discussing our recent engagement. So you can see why her having a boyfriend is a bit of a shock to me."

Alex quirked an eyebrow. "Engagement? You managed to get engaged in less than twenty-four hours to this Carlton-looking dude."

Mac wasn't sure if Alex meant for his comment to sound rude, but she didn't miss the crease in Dennis's forehead. Dennis was a good-looking man, but he didn't hold a candle to Alex.

"Actually, we aren't technically engaged yet," she said. "And I was going to mention it to you, Alex."

"Not engaged yet? Meaning you will be soon?" Alex asked, the vein in his neck peeking above the collar of his shirt. He stepped closer to her, pulling her into his embrace and disregarding the fact that Dennis was standing right there. His voice was low when he bent down to her ear. "Mac, come on. Is that really what you want? To marry this chump just to fulfill a pact?" She shivered again at the deep timbre of his voice. "There's no way he can make you feel the way I do. No way he can kiss you the way I do. Do the things to your body that I do."

"Alex," she said breathlessly. "I told you from the start that I'm not the relationship type. Dennis understands that and with him, I can fulfill the pact and keep things strictly business."

Alex frowned. "You mean, you can protect your heart from the possibility of getting hurt."

He was so close to the truth, Mac had to force herself to maintain a poker face. "Alex, I don't know what you want from me. You already knew I needed space."

"Yeah, space," he said. "But not enough space to get married to someone else in less than forty-eight hours."

Mac sighed. "I don't know what you want me to say."

Alex leaned back so that he could stare into her eyes. The hurt she saw there almost made her take back everything she'd said about needing space. Sometime during the intense eye exchange, Dennis had excused himself to wait for Mac inside the restaurant. Mac expected Alex to break the awkward silence, but apparently, he was done talking. She couldn't blame him. If she were him, she'd probably stop talking to her too.

"I have the team lined up for tomorrow to finalize Feng

Shuiing your office," Mac said, changing the subject. "I think you'll like the final touches we're adding to the cubicles."

"I was going to call you later tonight to tell you that I have to go out of town tomorrow and will be gone for a couple days."

Mac inwardly winced at the unexpected disappointment she felt. "That's fine. You don't have to be present tomorrow for the final touches. And no worries about our date in a couple days."

Alex was shaking his head before she finished her statement. "I'll be back in town this weekend. Pat mentioned that he and your mom are planning a party that they are calling Thanksmas. Whatever that means. Are you going?"

"Thanksmas is Thanksgiving and Christmas combined," Mac said with a laugh, grateful that some of the tension was broken. "At one point, my sis, mom and I were each living in different states, so we couldn't celebrate all the major holiday's together. My mom made up Thanksmas with basically combines two major holidays. Even though we're all in Boston, the name kinda stuck. But to answer your question, yes, I will be there."

"Great." His eyes grew even more serious. "Can you promise me that you won't get engaged to Dennis until after we've had a serious conversation about our relationship?"

"Of course," Mac said without hesitation. There was no way she could sign the agreement tonight. Not after running into the one man who made her question everything she thought about love.

Alex placed a soft kiss on her temple and turned to leave. Mac followed suit, already missing his lips on hers.

"Can I ask you one question before you go into the restaurant?" Alex asked.

Mac froze, but didn't face him. "Sure."

He didn't speak right away and she almost turned around to see if he was still standing there. "When you think about us together, does it make you happy? Can you picture a future ... with me?"

Mac knew that answering honestly would make the situation even more complicated, but Alex deserved a truthful answer. “Yes,” she said. “Thinking about us together often makes me happy and when I picture my future, it’s with you.”

Oh, great Mac. Could you sound any more confused? You’ve pictured a future with Alex, yet, you’re willing to marry another man? Her thoughts were bouncing around her mind like a ping pong ball.

Alex didn’t respond, but she felt his full lips softly kiss the back of her neck. As usual, she shivered beneath his touch. By the time she turned around, he’d already gone.

CHAPTER 9

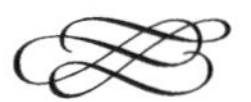

"Please tell me you didn't sign that contract last night Mac!"

Mac cringed at the sound of Quinn's high-pitched squeal.

"I didn't. I shouldn't have even told you the part about the contract." After last night, she'd awakened with a pounding headache. Once coffee and a pain reliever wouldn't work, she sent a text to her bestie squad for an emergency conference call.

"Well, I'm glad you did. However, next time, I'm making a rule against hiring husbands. Meaning, you can't do it!"

"What do you mean, next time?" Raven asked. "Quinn, it's bad enough that we all agreed to this pact in the first place. Let's refrain from any future best friend challenges that force us to walk down the aisle."

"I agree," Ryleigh added. "This shit is already giving me hives and we're only a few months in."

"Guys, I'm back," Ava said, returning to the call. "But, I have to jump off or else I'll keep putting you on hold. Mac sweetie, Alex is an amazing man and if there is even a small chance you're falling in love with him, then don't run from it. Follow your heart and remember that even though you have commitment issues, we all still love you."

Mac groaned into the phone after Ava hung up. "Ladies, I do not have commitment issues. At least not in the technical sense."

Quinn laughed. "What other way is there to take that?"

"You're shitting me, right," Ryleigh said.

"Yes, you do," Raven added.

"Listen, we don't have enough time to go through all your issues," Quinn said. "But like Ava said, we love you regardless. But Mac, at some point, you have to stop running from relationships. Every man isn't your ex, Prince. Every marriage won't end up like your parent's multiple marriages. And look at them now. They are both happy in their current marriages."

The line grew quiet, each woman apparently consumed by her own thoughts. "I really envy each of you," Quinn continued. "Love always seems to find the three of you even when you aren't searching. Ava too. But for me, I'm always searching for love, but can never find a man who loves me as much as I love him. I know this pact is insane, but guys, I crave love so bad, it hurts sometimes. So, even though I don't need you to verbally promise me anything on this call, just find it within yourselves to open your hearts to the possibility of finding your soul mate before the year is out. Not necessarily for the pact, but for yourselves. So you can experience the kind of love that each of you deserve whether you want it or not."

Quinn may have been the hopeless romantic of the group, but most of the time, her ideals on love made sense even if Mac and the others didn't want it to. "I understand," Mac said. Raven and Ryleigh agreed as well. "And we love you for always looking out for us Quinn. Your dream guy is out there, so don't worry too much about it."

"Maybe I'll break my own advice and hire a husband," Quinn said with a laugh. Pretty soon, all four women were laughing and Mac felt less tension in her body than she had before.

"Can I ask," Ryleigh said. "Are you falling for him?"

Mac bit her lip, wondering if she should tell them the truth, then concluding that she couldn't lie even if she wanted to. These were her besties. Her girlfriends. Her favorite people in the world. "Yes," she said after a brief pause. "I'm falling in love with him... pretty quickly. And it's scaring the shit out of me."

Quinn giggled. "I never thought I'd see the day that Mac *Queen of Friends with Benefits* would admit that she's falling in love. And since this is you we're talking about, I think it's safe to say that your feelings are even stronger than you're admitting, but I won't push for more info just yet."

Mac laughed as another thought popped into her mind. "Oh man, I forgot to mention the craziest shit that's happened. The former CEO of Alex's environmental engineer firm, who is also like a father to Alex, is none other than my mom's new husband. We found out the day they married."

"Shut up!" Quinn yelled.

"Holy shit," Ryleigh said.

Raven laughed. "Your life could be a sitcom right now."

As Mac filled them in on all the details, she thanked her lucky stars for having such a close group of friends who understood her better than most. Now, all she had to do was figure out how to handle her feelings for Alex before Thanksmas this weekend.

* * *

"NOPE, watching you stare a hole through Mac as you creepily hide behind my office window isn't stalker-ish at all."

Alex didn't even bother to turn to his brother Shane. "I already told you why I'm in here. Last time we saw each other, I told Mac I wouldn't be here when she placed the final touches in the office and with Mac, she doesn't react well to too many surprises in one week."

"Do you hear yourself?" Shane asked. "So, you thought hiding in my office and watching her through the blinds on my window was a better option?"

"Man, shut the hell up. Let me handle my woman and you focus on whatever flavor of the week you're dating right now."

Shane stood from his desk and walked over to where Alex was standing. "See, this is why I could never date only one woman. You like monogamy. I like… spreading the love." Shane laughed. "You don't even know what to do with yourself right now. I don't overlap my women, but why stress out or settle for one beautiful piece of ass when you can swim in a sea full of asses."

Alex shook his head. "Are you sure we're even related? How does swimming in a sea full of ass sound even remotely like a good time?"

Shane shrugged. "Some men like breasts. Others like legs. I like asses."

"I'm an ass man too, but that shit does not sound sexy," Alex said, taking another look at Mac. Today, she was wearing a deep green pencil skirt and navy blouse. As usual, her pumps matched her blouse and her ass looked so good, Alex almost bit his fist. Unlike last night, her curls were free-flowing, teasing her shoulders with every step she took.

Damn, I love this woman. Forget falling in love, Alex was already there. He finally released the blinds when he realized Shane was still staring at him with a knowing smile.

"What?"

"Oh, nothing," Shane said. "Except for the fact that you still haven't told me that I was right."

"Right about what?"

Shane shook his head. "About the fact that I told you the minute Mac was walking towards you at the bar at Owen and Ava's reception that you were going to give into temptation when it came to that woman. I didn't know you'd fall in love with her, but you have to admit that I was right."

"Fine," Alex said with a shrug. He hadn't verbalized to Shane that he was in love with Mac, but his brother knew him better than anyone and he was sure his love for her was obvious. "Shane, you were right."

"I know." Shane gave him a cheesy grin before his face grew serious. "And for the record, I'm proud of you for following your heart. Mom and dad would be proud of you too."

Alex slapped his hand over Shane's shoulder. "Thanks, that means a lot." He glanced back at the window. Although the blinds were closed, his heart beat quickened just knowing she was on the other side of the glass.

"Okay," Shane said as he slapped his hands together. "So, what's your plan? Because, don't take this the wrong way, but your girl Mac was a few minutes shy of agreeing to marry another man last night according to what you told me. And although I know you wouldn't have let that happen – and based off what McKenna told me, Mac has strong feelings for you too – you need a plan if you're going to convince Mac to be with you."

"I know." Alex thought back to the plan he'd concocted a few days ago. "But there's no way I'm losing that woman. And I'm damn sure not letting her marry another man. She's a runner. I knew that about her even before we started getting serious. But she can't run away from this. We're too good together. So, here's my plan."

Alex spent the next ten minutes telling his brother exactly how he planned on convincing Mac to give them a fighting chance. His only hope was that she didn't decide to attend the Thanksmas celebration wearing her running shoes.

CHAPTER 10

"What the hell are you doing here," Mac said to herself as she dropped her head on the steering wheel of her car. She'd been sitting outside of Alex's home for the past fifteen minutes and already, she'd seen a couple neighbors open their blinds and eye her suspiciously.

Forget the fact that it was eight o'clock at night, Mac had *never* waited outside of a man's home. Especially when he wasn't even home in the first place. She turned up the heat and leaned her head back on the head rest. "This is insane."

Mac really didn't have a good explanation as to why she was here. Earlier, when she'd been at his office with her team, she'd been disappointed that Alex wasn't there. Her friend and Alex's employee, Pete, had even questioned her about her relationship with Alex when she kept staring at his office, hoping that any second, he'd step out into the hallway and shoot her one of his devastatingly handsome smiles.

She glanced out into the empty, darkened street. "You're here because you miss him." She'd only known him for a few months, yet, she was already attached to seeing him. Talking to him. Kissing him. Making love to him. *Love.* There was that word again. It seemed the word was never far from her mind when it came to Alex. It was almost as if they were one in the same. *Guess this is how it feels to truly love a man.*

As a matter of fact, she wasn't sure if she ever really loved her ex because being with him felt nothing like it did with Alex. "And now, you're eerily waiting outside of his home for no reason other than the fact that you can't see him, so you might as well be near his home."

"Are you going to wait out here all night?" The knock on the window and sound of the voice on the other side of it caused her to squeal so loudly, that she wasn't surprised when those same neighbors who'd been watching her closely rushed back to their windows.

"Alex," she said as she pressed the button to roll down her window. "Do you make it a point to scare me half to death? What are you doing here?"

"I'm sorry," he said with a laugh. "But I should be asking you the same question. How long have you been out here in the cold?"

"Uh..." Her voice trailed off as she tried to think of an excuse. His black pea coat was unbuttoned and even though he was wearing a white tee, Mac could still make out the creases of his ab muscles. Her eyes made their way to his grey sweats and timberland boots before finally landing back on his face. She wasn't surprised to find him watching her intently, patiently awaiting her answer.

"I don't know why I'm here," she finally said. "And I thought you were out of town?"

"My meeting was rescheduled," he said.

"How did you know I was out here?"

He pointed to the camera's again.

"I forgot about the camera's."

"Plus," he said, amusement reflected in his eyes. "One of my neighbors called and said there was a woman outside my house and they weren't sure if you were talking to yourself, or on the phone."

"They did not," Mac said.

"They did." He laughed. "But I was hoping I'd see you before Thanksmas."

Mac squinted her eyes in observation. "Where you at the office today?"

Alex's lips curled to the side in a smile. "Yes, I was."

"Oh, okay." She was about to ask him why he didn't approach her, but he beat her to it.

"I was trying to give you space," he said. "But since you're here, why don't you come inside."

Mac glanced from the house, then back to Alex. She really did want to spend some more time with him. "Sure."

They walked to the house in silence. Once they were inside, Alex hung their coats in the closet in the foyer and they both removed their shoes.

"Do you want some hot chocolate?"

"Yes, that sounds good." She followed him to the kitchen and sat down on a stool at the island in the middle of the kitchen.

"Where you playing dice alone or with Daisy?" She asked, noticing a pair of dice sitting on the counter. At the sound of her voice, Daisy walked over to Mac and purred as she rubbed her fur against Mac's leg.

"Neither," Alex said as he pulled out two mugs and began boiling milk. "I had Shane and a few guys over the other night for poker and then a couple of the guys started shooting dice after."

Mac picked up the dice and began rolling them between her fingers. "Sounds like a good time."

"It was." Alex leaned against the counter, a sly look on his face. "I have an idea. How about you and I play a game."

Mac raised an eyebrow. "What kind of game?"

"Striptease dice," he said, taking a seat on the stool next to her. "If we roll an odd number, we remove a piece of clothing. If we roll an even number, we share something about ourselves that we haven't already shared."

Mac shifted in her seat, unsure if the butterflies in her stomach were from anxiousness or excitement. *Probably a bit of both.* She glanced down at her leggings and tank top. Her hands suddenly flew to her hair bun when she realized she hadn't even glanced in the mirror before she got in her car and headed to Alex's place.

"You look beautiful." Alex removed her hand from her hair. "You look amazing when you're all dolled up, but you look even more breathtaking all fresh-faced and casual, with your curls tossed on top of your head. I like you like this."

His penetrating stare immediately made her throat tighten. "Thank you," she said with a soft smile. She glanced back at the dice. "I've never played a striptease game, but I'm down."

Alex finished making their hot chocolate. "Do you want to go first?"

Mac shook her head. "You can go."

Alex picked up the dice and rolled an even and an odd number. "Okay," Alex said as he removed his socks. "Something you don't know about me... When I was in high school, I was part of a dance crew. We won a few local hip hop competitions, and now that I'm in my thirties, I still drag Shane to a street competition every now and then to check out the scene."

"Oh my God," Mac said with a laugh. "I so didn't peg you for a dancer."

"I've got moves." Alex stood and moon-walked across the kitchen floor. "Channing Tatum ain't got shit on me."

Mac was laughing so hard, she almost knocked over her hot chocolate. When she rolled the dice, she also received an odd and an even number. Taking her cue from Alex, she also removed her socks.

"Okay, so something you don't know about me is that one of my guilty pleasures is that I love to watch black and white romance movies. My infatuation is so bad, that I once drove for eight hours to another state just to attend a movie theater that was playing the classics all weekend."

Alex smiled. "I never would have guessed that. I haven't seen a black and white film in forever, so I guess you have to pick your favorite one day so we can watch it together."

Mac returned his smile. "I could do that." Alex rolled next and got two odd numbers. When he removed his white t-shirt and joggings pants leaving him with only his boxers on, her eyes stayed fixated on his every move. *His body is a work of art.* Finely sculpted as if he were chiseled just for her to watch and admire.

Mac took her turn next and rolled another odd and even number. She removed her shirt, glad that she'd decided to throw on a bra. Even though this game was for fun, Mac still hated to lose, so more clothes meant more turns.

"Hmm. Something else about me," she said, noticing the hungry look in Alex's eyes as he admired her black lace bra. "Although I'm an independent woman, I've never liked traveling out the country alone."

Alex studied her eyes. "Why is that? For safety reasons?"

"No, not really." Mac took a sip of her hot chocolate, letting the warm liquid slide down her throat before explaining. "I'm not sure it makes sense given the fact that I've chosen not to be in committed relationships all these years, but I always feel lonely when I'm traveling and I see couples wrapped up in their own love cocoon. Domestically, I'm usually fine. But internationally, it's more apparent to me. I guess I began feeling that way when I was in Barcelona for my twenty-seventh birthday. My sister McKenna was the only one who was able to make the trip with me, but I arrived three days before her.

"The first couple days of solo travel were fine, but the third day, it seemed everything that I'd signed up for, I was surrounded by people in love. I remember going on a wine tour with fourteen other people and I was the only one not coupled off. All the couples were nice and included me in conversation, but I recall the way that they kept stealing glances at one another with every stop we made. Some couples were on their honeymoon. One was celebrating an anniversary. Others were just vacationing."

"It probably felt like they didn't have a care in the world, right?" Alex asked.

"It did." Mac smiled as she thought about the people she'd met that day. "For most of my life I'd run from relationships, yet, that trip was the first time I'd wondered what it would be like if I had someone to love me like that. To look at me as if I was the only person who existed in his universe."

Mac looked at Alex, wondering why she'd chosen to share that piece of information about herself. *You know why,* her inner voice said. *You want him to be that person for you.*

Mac expected Alex to say something, but instead, he lightly grazed her hand with his before rolling the dice and landing on two even numbers. Sadness briefly flickered in his eyes before he spoke.

"After I lost my parents, I found it difficult to believe in love or anything resembling love for a while. It was hard to hold onto my faith when I felt like faith had slapped me in the face."

"That's understandable," Mac said as she leaned closer to him. "Anyone would feel the same way after suffering an unexpected loss."

"I know, but it wasn't just that." Alex ran his finger over the rim of his mug. "I was filled with so much anger back then, that I almost lost sight of myself. On the outside, people thought I was handling the loss well. And I kept up with the façade because I had to be strong for Shane. But on the inside, I was a fucking mess and so pissed that I actually walked into a church one day and cursed out the reverend."

Mac's eyes widened. "Had you attended the church and knew the reverend or was it a random church?"

"It was random. I'd just moved to Boston and was still so angry. So, I attended a service at a church I'd passed one day and an hour after it had ended, I was still sitting on the pew. When the reverend approached me, he'd barely gotten a word out before I just lost it. To this day, I think about how I'd yelled and cursed at him and I still feel guilty for my behavior. I was so beside myself and filled with emotions I didn't know how to handle. I still regret that day."

Mac squeezed his hand. "How did he respond to you?"

Alex smiled. "He sat there and let me get it all out. There were a couple people still in the church at the time and they listened too. No one said anything and I talked more that day than I had ever talked before. At the end, he took my hand in his and asked me to make him a promise. I thought it was the strangest reaction to my outburst, but I nodded almost immediately."

"What was the promise?"

Alex held her gaze. "He asked that I give myself enough time to grieve the loss and made me promise that when the time was right, to let love and faith back into my heart. My life."

The longing she saw in his eyes didn't surprise her, but the moment was so intense, she had to mentally remind herself to breathe. "And did you listen and take his advice?"

Alex grazed her bottom lip with the pad of his thumb. The move sent shivers down her spine. "It took a lot longer than I thought it would, but I finally took his advice a few months ago when this beautiful brown bombshell approached me at a bar and promised to give me a night I wouldn't forget." *Keep breathing Mac.* She was sure her heart was beating loud enough for Alex to hear.

"She sounds special," Mac said when she found her voice.

"She is." He trailed a finger along her collarbone. "And the crazy thing is, I'm not sure she has any idea how deep my feelings for her go."

"Infatuation does funny things to the heart." Mac let us a nervous giggle.

Alex shook his head. "Infatuation is a short-lived feeling that, although great and intense, cannot be the only emotion evoked between a man and a woman. Infatuation is a great start, but that phase can fade over time, so the real testament to love between a man and a woman is the foundation they build beyond sexual chemistry. What we have may have started physical, but it damn sure isn't the only reason I'm determined to make you mine. Mac, I'm usually a patient man. But let me clear up any confusion."

His voice got even deeper. "I'm as hypnotized by your mind as I am your body. And I want you. All of you. Hell, I want to consume your soul the way you've consumed me from the start, but for tonight, I'll take what you're willing to offer until you can decipher the feelings coursing through your body right now. But I'm not going anywhere. It took me too long to find you… a woman who's perfect for me in every way. I was starting to believe you didn't exist, but since you're right here, sitting in front of me looking every bit of sexy and determined not to fall as hard as I am, consider this your warning."

His jaw clenched as if he was so overcome with emotion, he could barely stand it. It was sexy as hell and had Mac not been hanging on his every word, she would have stripped her clothes off right then and there and told him he could do anything he wanted to her.

Mac opened her mouth, but no words came out. Alex glanced at her parted lips and closed the small distance between them, the dice game forgotten. When his lips touched hers, Mac moaned into the kiss.

Every part of her was overstimulated, but she didn't even care. No man had ever talked about her with such conviction in his voice before. Every part of her body felt as if it were on fire, his words scorching her insides in ways that his body would soon follow.

Alex lifted her and carried her to the large sofa in the living room, expertly removing the remainder of their clothes with a quickness she appreciated.

"I want to feel *all* of you," he said once they were both naked.

Mac didn't have to ask him what he meant. She felt the same urgency, but she was also slightly nervous.

"I'm on the pill and I get regular check-ups."

"I get check-ups as well," he said, dropping a quick kiss to her lips. "But we don't have to go bare if you aren't ready. I've actually never been bare before."

"Me neither," Mac said, taking a deep breath. She knew what she wanted. She didn't need any foreplay. She didn't want to play any games tonight. She was ready. She wanted Alex. All of Alex. There was so much more they needed to discuss, but she was all out of words tonight.

Pulling his head back down for a passionate kiss, she widened her legs, gasping into his mouth as he filled her inch by inch. He moved in slow, deliberate strokes, pushing her to the edge just to bring her back before she fell off the cliff.

The only noise in the entire room were their passionate moans and the crackling of wood burning in the fireplace. It hadn't even been long and Mac already felt her orgasm on the brink of releasing. She closed her eyes at the onslaught of pleasure. *This is what being with Alex would be like if you were together all the time. Exhilarating. All-consuming.* Mac was well aware of how she'd changed since she'd met Alex, but she was also having to constantly remind herself to live in the moment and not overthink the situation.

Throughout her entire life, Mac had always liked to be prepared for every situation. True, she enjoyed going with the flow at times, but Mac always had a plan. However, Alex hadn't been in her plans at all. When she thought about her future, love and marriage weren't two things that she often included. Yet, as Alex thrusted into her core, hitting her g-spot with every stroke, she was reminded that sometimes, plans altered despite your best abilities. And quite frankly, she wasn't even sure she wanted to revisit her old plans when the promise of new plans seemed so much brighter.

Mac didn't realize that tears were flowing down her cheeks

until she opened her eyes to look at Alex through her teary gaze. Alex kissed every one of her tears away, slowing his strokes in a way that made her cry aloud.

She wanted to close her eyes again, but she couldn't. Alex's eyes were trained on hers, and the emotion she saw in them captured her heart. He looked like he wanted to say something, but Mac slowly shook her head. She had a feeling she knew what he wanted to say, but she wasn't sure she could handle it.

As she continued to meet Alex stroke for stroke, she felt his gaze pierce through her remaining walls at the same time that her orgasm broke free. Alex followed soon after, never breaking eye-contact with her and Mac wasn't sure she'd ever seen anything sexier than the range of emotions flickering in Alex's eyes as he succumbed to the same passion she'd just experienced.

After a few seconds, Alex laid down beside Mac and pulled her to him. Mac wrapped her arms around Alex, more content than she'd ever been in her entire life. She was pretty sure she fell asleep with a smile on her face.

CHAPTER 11

"You're doing it again."

Alex reluctantly turned to his brother Shane. "What are you talking about?"

"You're doing that thing where you creepily stare at Mac. I don't think you've taken your eyes off her all night."

Alex looked back at Mac, ignoring Shane's words. He knew his brother was right. He'd been staring at her all night. It was becoming the norm for him.

In his defense, he hadn't seen her in three days and he was experiencing withdrawal. With Mac, he was noticing that she was his greatest addiction, which meant, if she was avoiding him – like she'd been throughout most of the Thanksmas celebration – he was probably going to be staring at her for the rest of the night.

At least when she'd been over a few days ago, she hadn't left before he'd awakened. Eventually, they'd made it to his bedroom and made love twice more before the sun rose. Waking up to Mac had been as perfect as he thought it would be and the only reason he'd let her out of bed was because they'd both had to go to work.

He'd thought they were finally done with her running from their relationship, but the minute he'd arrived at Thanksmas, Mac had kept her distance. In the back of his mind, he knew he should be used to her hot and cold ways when it came to him, but a man could only take so much. He wanted her. All of her. He'd told her so the other night and he wasn't willing to stand on the sidelines and give her a chance to meet someone else who wouldn't care for her the way that he cared for her.

"Dinner is ready," Marlene said to the group. He was sure that Mac wouldn't have chosen to sit across from him, but Pat and Marlene were at the heads of each table end, Shane had already chosen his seat, and McKenna took a seat across from Shane.

"So, McKenna," Shane said once they'd blessed the food and began eating. "Marlene was telling me about your bar the other day. I've heard from a few friends that it's one of the best in Boston. Apparently, it's known for its mac and cheese."

"We are," McKenna said with a proud smile. "I worked my butt off to open it and so far, it's doing great."

"Congrats." Shane flashed McKenna a crooked smile. "I'll have to check it out sometime."

"I'd love for you to check out my bar," McKenna said. "But this isn't going to happen." She waved her hand back and forth between her and Shane. Alex had to stifle a laugh at his brother's bewildered look.

"What do you mean? I wasn't flirting with you."

McKenna laughed. "You don't think I know your flirt smile? I saw it at Ava's wedding. I saw it at mom's wedding lunch. And I've seen it all night."

"I'm offended." Shane placed his hand over his chest. "I was just congratulating you." McKenna rolled her eyes at the same time Shane laughed.

Alex shook his head. "Real smooth Shane."

Shane shrugged. "In case you didn't know, McKenna and I are only flirting to break the tension between you and Mac."

"We are not flirting," McKenna said, waving her fork at Shane. Whether they were flirting or not, Shane was right. There was an unspoken tension at the table and Alex had no doubt that he and Mac were the cause. Apparently, Marlene was also curious about what was going on.

"How serious is your relationship?" Marlene asked as she looked up from her plate and glanced from Alex to Mac.

Alex opened his mouth to respond, but Mac was quick to answer. "We're taking things slow," she said.

Slow? He didn't know about Mac, but his feelings had developed quick and fast.

"Is that what we're doing?" He asked, not caring if their family heard. "Taking things slow?"

"I thought so," Mac said, her lips in a tightened line.

McKenna cleared her throat. "So, you're taking things slow, but you're serious about one another, right?"

Alex gave McKenna an appreciative smile. *At the end of all this, I really need to thank Mac's family.* They didn't know his plan, but they were helping without even realizing it.

"We care about each other," Mac said, looking down at her plate.

"You care for me?" Alex asked. "That's all?" He was pushing his luck by putting her on the spot in front of everyone, but it couldn't wait. He had to know.

"I care for you a lot," she said, finally looking at him.

Alex pushed further. "Just a lot, huh?"

Mac sighed. "I'm not sure why you're pushing this tonight."

"I'm just trying to understand," Alex said. "Do you only care for me, or are your feelings stronger?"

"Alex."

He heard the warning in her voice, but he wasn't going to back down. "Baby, I just want to make sure we're on the same page. That's all. I know it seems like I'm pushing you, but I need you to vocalize the feelings you've shown me, but haven't said aloud."

She raised her arms in frustration. "What do you want me to say, Alex? Do you want me to say that I've loved you for a while now? That I probably fell that first night we spent together. That I left that one morning because the night before had been so incredible, that I couldn't imagine you walking out of my life. That a few nights ago had meant even more to me than all the others. That the thought of never being with you again makes my heart ache so badly, I can barely stand the feeling. That until you, I never knew I could love someone so much and not dwell on what the future holds, but live in the moment instead. Are those the things you want me to say?"

His lips curled to the side in a smile. "That's a good start," he said. "Especially since I'm sure you want to hear that I love you just as much, if not more. That I knew the moment you approached me at Owen and Ava's wedding, I would never want another woman. That the day you walked into my office, my brain was already concocting a plan to see how I could keep you in my life. That until you, there has never been a woman who has impacted me so much."

He rose from his seat and walked over to Mac's side of the table. Reaching in his pocket, he pulled out a three-caret diamond ring and got down on one knee. "Would you want to hear that before we even had our first official date, I knew you were my future, so I purchased this ring and planned on proposing to you when the time was right?"

At her gasp, he continued. "Mackenzie Cannon, you challenge me in ways I've never been challenged, and in case you didn't know, I am deeply and unconditionally in love with you. I'd be ready to get married tomorrow if we could plan a wedding that fast. But I won't ask you the question I've been dying to ask you unless you're ready to hear it. I'm showing you this ring and kneeling on one knee because I'm ready to propose now and I wanted you to know that it wasn't because of some pact I just found out about. It's because I fell in love with you the minute I laid eyes on you."

By the end of his speech, she was shaking. "This is crazy," she said with tears in her eyes. "There is still so much for us to learn about each other. What if you wake up one day and you regret your decision?"

"I'll never regret marrying you." He placed a soft kiss on the back of both her hands. "Mac, can't you tell that I'm completely infatuated with you and that feeling is not a today kind of feeling. Or a tomorrow kind of feeling. It won't go away next year. Or a decade from now. Hell, even when I'm in my grave, my heart will still belong to you."

Her eyes lit up when she touched the ring. "Are you sure?"

"Mac, listen to me. I would have married you after that night we shared at Owen and Ava's wedding if I hadn't thought you'd run in the opposite direction. Sometimes, when you know, you know. You're it for me. You're the woman I want to spend the rest of my life with. All you need to do is take a chance and trust me. In fact, you can retire all but one pair of your gym shoes because I refuse to let you run away again." He studied her eyes. "Unless you don't feel as strongly about me..."

* * *

MAC'S HEART was beating so loudly, she could barely hear her own thoughts. Marrying Alex after only a few months seemed like a ridiculously short amount of time and yet, her gut was telling her that this was it. This was the man she'd been waiting her entire life for. He was the reason she'd had casual flings instead of giving her heart away. She'd been saving her heart, saving her love, for *him*. She'd been waiting for Alex to arrive and the part that she still couldn't get over was the fact that she'd been the first one to seek him out at the wedding reception.

Mac closed her eyes to try and hold back the tears that were brimming her eyelids. *A real woman knows when it's time to stop fighting and just let go. Always be a real woman, Mac. Never be the type of woman who's scared to take a chance on life... on love.*

Grandma Pearl had given her so much advice, but right now, those words were standing out loud and clear. She knew what she had to do, and as crazy as it was, she'd never felt more confident in her decision.

"I am so in love with you, Alexander Carter. You make me a better woman and I know that if you ask me the question that you're dying to ask and that I'm dying to answer, I'll spend the rest of our lives showing you just how much you truly mean to me."

His Kool-Aid grin reached from ear-to-ear. "Mackenzie 'Mac' Cannon, I would love nothing more than if you would do me the honor of being my wife. Will you finally put me out of my misery and marry me?"

She grinned as the tears she'd been holding back finally released. "Yes, Alex. I'll marry you."

Alex had barely placed the ring on her finger before he pulled her from her seat and placed a passionate kiss on her lips. She drowned out their cheering family as she kissed her soon-to-be husband. A part of her was still in disbelief that she was going to marry the man she'd always dreamt about but never thought she would have.

"Did you mean what you said?" she asked when they broke the kiss. "About getting married soon. Would you be okay with that?"

He flashed her a sly smile. "Of course, I meant it. My baby's not missing out on a bet when all she has to do is marry me sooner so that I can permanently take her off the market. Your little teal book is pretty thick."

Her eyes widened. "You found my little teal book?"

"Not on purpose," he said. "You left me at your place that one morning and the note you wrote me was sitting on top of it."

"That's right," she said with a laugh. "What will I do with all those numbers now that I'm practically a married woman?"

"We'll have a ritual before we toss it in the fire," Alex said with a laugh. When he leaned down to capture her in another kiss, Mac let the remainder of her tears fall down her cheeks. What she'd thought was only a temporary fixation on the best man at her friend's wedding turned out to be the man she planned on spending forever with. She guessed the good ole' saying was true… love always finds you when you least expect it.

EPILOGUE

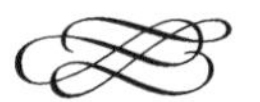

Six Weeks Later

"I CAN'T BELIEVE you're getting married," Quinn said as she helped button the back of Mac's wedding dress. "Even crazier, I can't believe you're the first one to fulfill the pact and win the best friend challenge."

"Me neither," Mac said with a smile. "Every day for the past six weeks, I've awakened with a delicious kiss from Alex and a reminder of how many days until I was Mrs. Mackenzie Carter."

Ava passed Mac her veil. "I can't believe one of Owen's best friends is marrying one of my best friends."

"I know right," Mac said. "That gives me an excuse to visit you in Rosewood more."

"I plan on visiting home more, too," Ryleigh said.

"Maybe we should all try and visit Rosewood a couple times a year," Raven suggested. "Spending time together at Ava and Owen's wedding was great, but it wasn't nearly long enough." Each woman nodded her head in agreement.

McKenna joined the group. "Grandma Pearl would be so proud of you," she said as she handed Mac a small box.

"What's this?" Mac asked.

McKenna pointed to the box. "Open it and see." Mac opened the box, her hands shaking as she picked up the beautiful blue sapphire ring.

"It's Grandma's fortieth anniversary ring that Grandpa gave to her years ago," McKenna said. "It's for your something old and something blue."

Mac placed her hand over her chest. "I haven't seen this ring in years. I had no idea that you had it."

"I may or may not have had to go to Texas last weekend and threaten a few cousins to see who had it. Everyone knows that Grandma would have wanted you to have her ring."

Mac pulled McKenna in for a hug. "Thank you, sis, now my day is perfect."

"Well maybe this will make it even better." McKenna removed her charm bracelet from her wrist and placed it on Mac's wrist. "Now you have something borrowed."

"Beautiful," Mac said, kissing McKenna on the cheek.

"Mackenzie, may I come in?" All the ladies turned at the sound of a knock on the door.

"Of course, you can, Mom."

Marlene opened the door and paused when her eyes landed on Mac. "Sweetie, you look stunning."

"Thanks, Mom," Mac said as she did a quick twirl in her lace asymmetrical wedding gown. "I was hoping you would be back before it was time for me to walk me down the aisle."

These past few weeks had been a whirlwind of wedding planning, but it had also brought her and her mother even closer together. Mac had finally opened up to her mother about how Marlene's previous relationships had impacted her view on love. In return, Marlene had told Mac how hurt she was that her actions had transformed Mac's view on relationships.

In the end, Mac also realized that she'd wrongfully judged her mother based off of what the men in her life had done and not on her own merit to overcome those adversities. Rick had helped Mac see her fault with that issue. Turns out, he wasn't such a bad guy after all and Mac had all the confidence in the world that her mother and Rick would last for the long haul.

Mac had also had a long conversation with her dad, Ike, and he'd admitted that he never should have painted Marlene in such a bad light when Mac and McKenna were younger. He was the one who originally hurt their marriage by betraying Marlene's trust. Marlene was just trying to protect not only her heart, but her daughters as well. Mac found it funny that the one thing she always ran from was now one of the qualities she admired about both of her parents. They never gave up on finding love and Mac loved them unconditionally.

"Ladies, how about we give them some privacy," McKenna said as she ushered out the other bridesmaids.

"Oh, I almost forgot." McKenna rushed over to the corner of the room and grabbed Mac's gym shoes.

"Why are you taking my gym shoes?" Mac asked.

McKenna shrugged. "Your future husband asked me to bring them to him. Probably afraid you'll run."

Mac laugh. "Well you tell the groom that I'm done running, so he can stop hiding all my gym shoes."

"I can't promise he'll listen, but I'll tell him," McKenna said with a smile.

"My precious daughter," Marlene said when they were alone. She lightly cupped Mac's face in her hands. "Have I told you how amazing you are and how proud I am to be your mother?"

Mac sniffed. *Don't cry, Mac, you'll mess up your makeup.* "Have I told you how much I admire and respect you?" Mac swiped a fallen tear from her cheek. "And I'm immensely proud to be your daughter."

"I brought you something." Marlene handed Mac a red velvet box. "I hope you like it. It's for your something new."

Mac opened the beautiful box and removed the locket that was inside. On one side was a picture of Marlene and McKenna. On the other, was a picture of Mac and Grandma Pearl.

"I love it," Mac said as she pulled her mother in for a hug. "Thank you, Mom."

"You're welcome, sweetie." They didn't stop hugging until McKenna knocked on the door and informed them that it was time to walk down the aisle.

The décor in the chic Boston hotel was everything Mac had hoped it would be. Especially for a wedding that was planned in a short amount of time.

"Just breathe, sweetie. You'll do fine."

"Thanks, Mom," Mac said as she placed a kiss on her cheek.

"And don't forget," Mac's dad said as he came to stand beside her in the hallway. "If it doesn't work out, you can always find love again."

"Oh, Ike hush," Marlene said as she swatted him on the shoulder. "Alex is Mackenzie's one true love. They're in it for the long haul."

"As long as Mac is happy, I'm happy." Ike kissed Mac's cheek. "You look beautiful. Come on baby girl. It's almost time."

Mac's nerves were rattled until she heard the first cords of Etta James singing "At Last", the song she was walking down the aisle to, which also happened to be her grandmother's favorite.

As Mac walked down the aisle, gazing into the eyes of the man she loved, she realized that for the first time in her life, everything was *perfect*. There was no doubt that marriage would be hard work and would take a lot of good communication, but she knew in her heart that she and Alex had what it took to make it work.

I love you, Alex mouthed as she got closer to him. Even though she didn't think her heart could melt any more for this man, it dissolved into a puddle right then and there.

Her mind drifted to the last conversation she'd had with Grandma Pearl. *It is far easier for a husband and wife to build a life together when they follow the same blueprint. Let your similarities form the foundation of the blueprint for your future while your differences serve as the tools needed to alter the blueprint to what works best for you and your family. Mac, promise me when you find that special someone, you won't let fear hold you back. You'll let go of your insecurities and allow him to love you the way you deserve to be loved.*

Mac sighed, unable to hold back the tears. When she'd made that promise to Grandma Pearl, she'd admit that she hadn't planned on following through with it.

She may have subconsciously used the ruse of the wedding pact she'd made with her friends as a way to open her heart, but regardless of the circumstances that allowed her to let her guard down, Mac had gotten the best gift of all... A man who didn't expect her to be anyone but herself and loved her unconditionally. She was ready for their future. She was ready to design their blueprint.

Taking a deep breath, she briefly closed her eyes and relished the moment she'd finally release her remaining reservations on love. Her future started now and she couldn't wait to see what happened next. *Ready. Set. Let go.*

ONCE UPON A BRIDESMAID SERIES

I hope you enjoyed YOURS FOREVER! Make sure you check out the remaining books in the series!

Also, authors love to hear from readers! Thanks in advance for any reviews, messages or emails :).

Once Upon A Bridesmaid Blurb:

When four bridesmaids come together to support their best friend's wedding, they realize that most of the people they know have already tied the knot. Whether unlucky in love or single by choice, these besties make a pact to change their relationship status. The goal is simple... Each woman has one year to find Mr. Right and say 'I do'. Between passionate one-night-stands and best friend hookups, these bridesmaids are in for a wild ride. Are they in over their heads? Or will one impulsive wedding pact change their lives… forever.

Yours Forever by Sherelle Green (Book 1)

Beyond Forever by Elle Wright (Book 2)

Embracing Forever by Sheryl Lister (Book 3)

Hopelessly Forever by Angela Seals (Book 4)

HIGH CLASS SOCIETY SERIES

All 4 Novellas in HCS Series Coming Soon

In a society of trust fund babies, millionaires and upper-class peers, four women seeking a prestigious ivy league education were thrust into a privileged world of wealth and aristocrats. Overwhelmed by the segregation they witnessed in the university that forced students to date within their own social class, they decide to create a world not based on society's rules. An organization in which the everyday woman not given the chance to date a person of caliber can overcome the barriers placed before her and date whomever she pleases.

There are no limits to finding love and they simply supply women the tools and encouragement to go after the person they want in hopes that it results in a successful relationship. Hence, after graduating from college in 2006, High Class Society Incorporated was established. Now, years later, although all four founding women have established successful careers, the secret organization is in full effect. But like every secret society, the biggest obstacle is keeping it a secret.

Blue Sapphire Temptation by Sherelle Green (Book 1)

Her Sweetest Seduction by Angela Seals (Book 2)

Sealed with a Kiss by Angela Seals (Book 3)

Passionate Persuasion by Sherelle Green (Book 4)

MEET LOGAN "LO" AND TRISTAN

COMING SOON: Check website for latest updates!

Logan "Lo" Sapphire has never backed down from a challenge, so she's convinced that she can persuade the stern and unyielding self-made millionaire to keep High Class Society a secret after he bursts into her office demanding to know his sister's whereabouts. The last thing Lo wants to do is go on a wild goose chase with a walking sex ad to find his sister, but maybe, just maybe, finding her will coax him into signing a confidentiality agreement.

Tristan Derrington has a reputation for doing what he wants, when he wants. Usually nothing will stop Tristan from pursuing a gorgeous beauty like Logan, but even temptation in four-inch heels won't stand in the way of him finding his sister and exposing HCS. He may think he has a solid plan to avoid their obvious attraction, but even the best laid plans can fail. The more time they spend together, the harder it is to deny their explosive chemistry. Especially when they realize how delicious giving into temptation can be.

EXCERPT: BLUE SAPPHIRE TEMPTATION

Prologue

January 2006

Yale University

"That's it! I'm done wasting my time on these snobbish boys who think more with their wallets than their minds."

Logan Sapphire looked up from her notebook as her friend Harper Rose entered their apartment.

"I'm guessing the date didn't go well."

Harper huffed. "Let's try terrible. Horrible. Possibly the worst date of my entire life."

"Maybe you're forgetting about that frat guy you went out with two months ago," said their other roommate, Peyton Davis, as she entered the living room and took a seat on the chair opposite Logan. "If I remember correctly, he rushed your date because he had to take out that freshman and he actually had the nerve to tell you that."

"Oh right," Harper said as she kicked off her heels and plopped on the couch. "Yeah, he was pretty bad."

All three ladies glanced at the door as their fourth roommate, Savannah Westbrook, entered the apartment lugging a book bag, tote bag, and laptop bag that she immediately dropped at the entrance. Logan never did understand why Savannah always carried around so much stuff, but that was Savannah. She was always researching, studying, or doing something that required her to take her notes, books and laptop everywhere.

"What did I miss?" Savannah asked as she sat on the couch next to Harper.

Harper sighed. "Just me ranting about my sorry excuse for a date with that arrogant jerk I went out with tonight."

"Wait, isn't he that fine guy from your photo journalism class that you were dying to go out with? I thought he seemed different than the others."

"They're all the same," Harper replied. "Not only did he spend most the night talking about himself, his money, and his dad's company that he was going to be working at right after graduation. But then he had the nerve to slip me a key card for the hotel room he'd booked for the night."

"What did you tell him?" Logan asked. Harper was the insightful one in the group so there was no doubt in her mind that Harper tried to explain to him exactly why he was an arrogant jerk instead of just cursing him out. She was the one who didn't just take things from surface value, but instead, she always took a deeper look.

"He told me that most women would jump at the opportunity to have sex with him on a first date. So I told him all the reasons why he would never get into my panties."

"The nerve of these guys. See, this is the only reason why I regret not going to a regular university. There are some real pretentious assholes here," Peyton chimed in.

"And even if you're lucky enough to find a *trust fund* guy here who is actually decent, you run into issues with his friends and family accepting you," Logan added. Although she was currently engaged to one of those *privileged* men and had been dating him for most of college, she couldn't help that feeling in the pit of her stomach. That feeling that warned her she was making the wrong decision by marrying him after college and joining a family that didn't accept her or think she was worthy enough to carry their last name. She didn't date him for his money, but his family didn't see it that way.

"We aren't the only women with these issues," Savannah stated. "Just last week, I was talking to perky Paula, who couldn't stop crying in class after her boyfriend of three years broke up with her."

Logan shook her head in disbelief. "They were so in love. Please tell me it's not because her family had to file for bankruptcy."

"You guessed it," Savannah confirmed. "Apparently, being with someone who no longer has money isn't a good look. Three years down the drain."

"See, I worked my ass off to get here," Harper said. "Being from a low or middle-class family shouldn't make me less worthy of love than someone born from money. Isn't love about finding your soul mate and the person you want to spend the rest of your life with? Wouldn't you rather have a hardworking woman by your side, money or no money?"

Peyton leaned over and slapped hands with Harper. "Agreed. And the opening line on a date shouldn't be how much my family makes or how dating me can improve or decrease their social status."

Logan glanced around at her friends as they began sharing stories that they'd heard around campus from women who had fallen for a guy only to realize that because of social status, they couldn't be together. Logan and her roommates were all from hard-working families and each had worked hard to get accepted into Yale on scholarship and follow their dreams. They didn't major in the same discipline, but they'd instantly connected during freshman orientation week and had been close all through college. Even though it was their last semester, she was certain they would remain friends after graduation and already, the foursome was planning on moving to New York together.

"You know what's crazy," Logan said finally closing her notebook and placing it on the coffee table. "We each gained so much by attending Yale, but I think you all agree that we've never faced this much adversity when it came to dating and by the sound of it, there are so many ladies on campus that are in the same boat as we are. And not just here at Yale, I'm sure this is an issue outside of school as well."

Harper nodded her head in agreement. "I think you're right. My cousin went through a similar issue with liking a man she met at a business conference. She said he was really interested in her as well, but after spending the first two conference days together, he was pulled in several different directions by other women."

"So he just stopped talking to her?" Logan asked.

"Sort of. See, at her company she's an executive assistant, which is a great position and she really loves it. She accompanied the president of her company on the trip. But the women approaching the man she was interested in were all VP's, Presidents of other companies or women who were part of a family that sponsored the conference. Since his organization was planning the conference, his job as CEO of the event was to wine and dine all clients to try and get new business."

Logan began seeing the bigger picture. "So basically, he was interested, but because of obligations to talk to the other women, he couldn't spend as much time with her."

"That's right. But I told her that I felt like she should have just continued to talk to him like she had been. She wasn't invited to every event at the conference, but she was invited to enough where she could have pushed past those women and made an effort."

"Easier said than done," Savannah said. "It's one thing to know a man is interested. It's another issue entirely to have the confidence not to care about what the other people in attendance think and convince yourself that you're bold enough to talk to him."

"I agree with Savannah," Peyton said. "Sometimes it's about self-confidence and the idea that you aren't any different than the other women vying for his attention. All men who have money or were born from money don't only want to date women from influential families. We run into that a lot here at Yale, but I guess we have to keep in mind that we are dealing with boys trying to be men. Not men who already know what they want and don't care about what others think."

"Those men are out there," Logan added with a sly smile. "We just have to find them."

Harper squinted her eyes at Logan. "Lo, I know that look. What are you thinking?"

"Do you guys remember last year when we were sitting around drinking wine after celebrating Savannah's twenty-first birthday?"

They all nodded their head in agreement. "Do you remember what we discussed that night?"

Savannah scrunched her head in thought. "Was that the time we stayed up all night discussing what it would be like in a world that didn't have typical dating rules that you had to follow? I think we talked about how it would be if we could date good men and not worry about whether or not money, family names, or social standing would be an issue."

"Exactly," Logan said snapping her fingers. "Peyton, you said you would love it if we could start our own organization. Then Harper, you started talking about how great it would be if it were a secret organization that no one knew about. Then Savannah, you and I started talking about the way the organization could work and how great it would be if we also encouraged women to pursue love and help build their self-esteem. Especially if their self-esteem was damaged as a result of a bad relationship."

"Um, so what exactly are you getting at?" Peyton asked inquisitively. "Because it sounds a lot like you're trying to say we should turn the ideas we had that day into reality."

Logan smiled and clasped her hands together as she looked at each roommate.

"Oh no," Savannah said shaking her head. "That's precisely what you're trying to say isn't it?"

"Come on guys, you all have to admit that our ideas that night were pretty amazing."

"I'm pretty sure I was tipsy," Harper mentioned.

"No you weren't. We had just started drinking our first glass when we talked about this." Logan got up from her chair and began pacing the room as her brain began working overtime.

"Hear me out ladies. Peyton, you have amazing business sense and there is no doubt in my mind that you have what it takes to handle the ins and outs of a secret organization. Savannah, you're amazing at researching and like we discussed last year, it would be great if we could develop profiles of eligible bachelors, but they have to be the right type of men. Harper, you're a wiz with marketing and social media. Private or not, we will definitely need that. And of course, since I'm majoring in human resources, I could handle meeting and conversing with the members."

She turned and was greeted with blank stares from all three women, so she continued talking. "I know we would have to work out a lot of kinks and really solidify our business plan, but there is no doubt in my mind that we were on to something great the night of Savannah's birthday and I'm sure, if we put our minds to it, we could create something amazing. A secret society unlike any other."

When their faces still displayed blank stares, she'd thought maybe she was talking too fast and they hadn't heard her. She was relieved when Harper's mouth curled to the side in a smile.

"I can't believe I'm saying this, but I honestly loved the idea when we first came up with it last year, and I love it even more now that we're graduating. Off hand, I can already think about several women who would be more than happy to join."

"So, we're really going to do this?" Savannah said with a smile. "We are actually going to start our own secret society?"

"Not just any society," Peyton said as she stood to join Logan. "Didn't we create some guidelines for the organization that night?"

"I think I have all our notes from that," Logan said as she ran to her room to grab her laptop and returned to the living room. She kneeled down at the coffee table, opened up a word document, and was joined by Harper, Savannah and Peyton who kneeled down around her laptop as well.

"Here it is. All our notes from that night."

Savannah pointed to sentence. "Oh wow, it says here that we thought members should have to take a rigorous personal, professional and spiritual assessment when they join before they are placed in a position to meet quality matches."

Harper pointed to another sentence. "And here it says that we will build well-researched profiles on eligible bachelors and give women the tools and encouragement to go after the man of their dreams."

"So we decided that this wouldn't be a match making service right?" Peyton asked the group. "We would place women in a position to meet a man they are interested in, but we aren't playing matchmaker and setting them up on a date."

"That seems accurate to what we discussed," Logan answered. "But of course, we'll have to get all those details nailed down before inviting members."

"Didn't we come up with a name too?" Peyton asked searching the notes on the page.

Logan scrolled down until she landed on the page she was searching for.

"High Class Society Incorporated," she said aloud to the group. "That was the name we created last year."

Harper clasped her hands together. "Oh I remember now! I still love that name."

"Me too," Savannah and Peyton said in unison.

Logan pointed her finger to the words on the screen written underneath the name of the organization and read them aloud. "There are no limits to finding love, no rulebook to discover your soul mate, and no concrete path to follow in order to reach your destiny. In High Class Society, we make that journey a little easier. High Class Society … where elite and ordinary meet."

She looked up at each of the ladies, each with a knowing gleam in their eyes. This year didn't just mark their graduation and start of their careers. It also marked the beginning of a new chapter for the four of them. A chapter that was sure to be filled with pages and pages of new self-discoveries

Chapter 1

9 years later...

"You have *one* minute to tell me where the hell my sister is, or I'll have no choice but to call the authorities and expose this disgraceful ass company."

The deep timbre in the man's voice bounced off the burgundy walls of the Manhattan office and teased Logan's ears. Her big, doe-eyes stared at the sexy intruder with the rich, mocha skin tone as she tried her best not to drop her mouth open in admiration. She knew who he was. Her company had done their research on him when Logan had first met his sister. They were actually in the process of gathering further information on him to build a more solid profile and add him to their list of exceptional men. However, the pictures definitely didn't do this former Canadian turned New Yorker justice.

In the profile she'd received from her partner and friend,

Savannah Westbrook, the Director of Research and Development for High Class Society, she could tell he was a walking sex ad. Even after recognizing his clearly masculine sex appeal, she couldn't have prepared herself for the onslaught of pleasure she'd feel coming face-to-face with temptation.

Her eyes wandered up and down the length of his body that was encased in a deep-blue Tom Ford suit, complementing leather shoes, and a classic navy-blue watch with gold trimmings. Licking her lips as she admired his six-foot frame, she tried not to imagine how enticing he'd look without a stitch of clothing on. Usually Logan was attracted to men with curly hair and a caramel complexion, but the man standing before her didn't have either of those qualities ... and damned if she even cared. Within a few seconds, she'd dismissed every physical characteristic she'd ever believed she wanted in a man. *Delicious,* she thought after taking note of his short fade and chiseled jawline, his neatly groomed features mirroring that of a Tyson Beckford look-alike rather than Shemar Moore.

"I'm so sorry, Lo," said her assistant, Nina, a grad student at Columbia University, as she came rushing in to the office behind the unwelcomed guest. "I'm not sure how he even got clearance into the building or how he found your office."

"It wasn't hard to find your office with so few people here and a distracted security guard," he explained, his eyes never straying from Logan. His piercing gaze was so intense that Logan was glad she was sitting at her desk or she would have surely faltered. "And you should really lock up the bathroom window in the basement. I climbed right in."

She tilted her head to the side, unable to believe that a man of his status would climb through a window to get into their office.

"It's okay, Nina," she reassured, refusing to break their stare-down. "I'll listen to what Mr. Derrington has to say."

Nina hesitantly exited the office and left the door cracked, instead of closing it all the way like she normally would when Logan had a meeting.

"Ms. Sapphire, I take it that you already know who I am," he stated with a slight curl of his lips. *Don't do that,* she thought when he walked a little closer to her desk. His imposing stance was already sending her body into a frenzy. She couldn't stay seated and let him have the upper hand.

"It appears you already know who I am as well, Mr. Derrington." Rising from her seat, she noted the appreciative glance he shot in her direction. She smoothed out her designer skirt and blouse before sitting on the edge of her desk. His eyes ventured to her creamy, maple thighs before making their way to the swell of her breasts.

Logan's breath caught as she watched him observe her. She was hardly showing any cleavage and her clothes were concealing all of her assets. Yet the way he was staring at her, made her feel as if she wasn't wearing anything at all. The air around them was thick with awareness, and the silence almost caused her to fidget under his stare.

"I've been away on business and came back early because I hadn't heard from my younger sister. So I went to her condo, and imagine my surprise when I surfed her laptop, trying to find some information about her whereabouts, and saw several screen shots saved in a folder on her desktop entitled High Class Society Incorporated."

Logan winced at his statement, silently cursing his discovery. HCS prided themselves on being paperless, a key to keeping the organization a secret. Unfortunately, no matter how good their small IT team was, some things were hard to avoid … like members taking screen shots containing information that couldn't get out to the public.

"Ms. Sapphire, after I got over the shock of an organization like yours existing, I researched the duties of the founders listed on one of the screen shots and realized that you may be the only person to know where my sister is. According to what I read, all women are supposed to check in daily with you if they're away with a prospect, correct?"

"That is true," Logan responded. "May I remind you that the contents on those screen shots are private, and my organization did not approve for your sister to go off on her own before finishing part two of her orientation session, including our policy on safety."

"So she *is* with a man," he said more to himself than her. His jaw twitched and he placed both hands in his pockets, frustration radiating from his body. "May I remind *you* that as long as my sister is missing, everything is my business. She wouldn't have gotten this idea to run off with God knows who if your company didn't exist."

"We help women find the person of their dreams, Mr. Derrington. We have rules, which she didn't follow. We aren't babysitters."

"I assume I don't need to reinforce that I'll sue you for all your worth if you don't tell me what I need to know, Ms. Sapphire … if that's even your real last name."

"It is," she stated firmly. "I have nothing to hide, and although this is against my better judgment, I will tell you who she's with," she continued, purposely leaving out the fact that she didn't know where Sophia was. She did have something to hide, but she needed to bluff to buy her and her partners some time before he went to the authorities.

"So," he said, removing both hands from his pockets and waving them for her to explain, "who is my sister with?"

Logan sighed, still not okay with sharing the information, but she knew he wasn't leaving without an answer. "She's with social media prodigy, Justice Covington."

She watched all of the color drain from his face while both hands curled into fists. His breathing grew heavier and he slowly rolled his neck … purposeful … measured. Logan found her own breathing growing labored as she sat and watched a range of emotions cross his face.

“Then we definitely have a problem,” he stated as he released his fists and leaned in closer to her, “because Justice Covington met my sister when she was eighteen and they tried to get married two years ago. If we don’t find them, he may finally get his wish ... *if* they haven’t tied the knot already.”

***

30 minutes earlier ...

“Where are you?” Logan Sapphire asked aloud as she scrolled through the online files she had for one of the newest clients to High Class Society, Sophia Derrington. Her cherry-colored office desk—that was usually extremely organized—was covered in an array of paperwork and maps she’d printed to try and piece together where Sophia might be. In all of her eight years of being Director of HR and Recruiting, she’d never lost contact with a client for this long.

“What the hell am I going to do?” she huffed aloud, standing up and running her French tipped fingernails through her thick and wavy copper-colored hair. She paced back and forth in her office, glad that her partners had all retired for the night. Only Logan and her assistant remained, and she was extremely thankful that Nina had decided to help her search for Sophia, despite the fact that Nina felt partially responsible.

Sophia hadn’t been born from wealth, but thirty-four-year-old Tristan Derrington, Sophia’s older brother, was a self-made millionaire and one of the most sought after custom watch designers in the country. He created top-notch designs for numerous celebrities, singers, hip-hop artists, and political figures. High Class Society had certain rules, and one of them was to ensure that the only women allowed in the society were women who weren't born from money or from highly privileged families. They were all successful professionals and entrepreneurs, or self-made millionaires. Of course, sometimes rules were meant to be broken, and in some instances, they made an exception and allowed a woman to join who was born from money or a well-known family. Those situations were handled on a case-by-case basis.

Even though it seemed unfair, Logan and her partners had strict rules that they had to adhere to in order to ensure that High Class Society was successful and effective. They didn't just let any woman into the organization. Each woman went through a psychological, spiritual, and professional screening to ensure that they were truly looking for love and not a gold-digging groupie. Their clientele consisted of women of different nationalities, ethnic backgrounds, and occupations, and they were proud of the successful relationships that had developed from their company.

Logan stopped pacing and abruptly sat down in her desk chair, accidently knocking over a cup of black coffee as she did so. "Shit," she cursed, quickly grabbing some nearby napkins and dabbing up the coffee.

"Are you okay?" Nina yelled from outside of her office.

"I'm fine," she yelled back after she'd wiped up most of the coffee and waved the wet stained paperwork in the air to dry it quicker.

Focus, Logan! she thought to herself as she leaned back in her chair and clasped her hands in her lap. *Are there any clues in the last conversation you had with Sophia?*

Ever since she'd first met Sophia months ago, the twenty-four year old had wormed her way into Logan's heart after divulging the story about how she'd lost the only man she had ever loved and was ready to see what else was out there. She'd claimed she needed High Class Society, and Logan had chosen to ignore the signs that something more was going on. Now that she had no idea where Sophia had run off to, she had time to reflect on the fact that Sophia had only shown interest in one man ... Justice Covington. HCS always listed possible matches in each woman's personal online folder and Sophia had included other men in her profile as "persons of interest," but any time Logan had spoken with Sophia, the young lady had only asked her about Justice, the thirty-two-year-old brain behind an up and coming social media network.

Closing her eyes, she thought back to the information she'd given Sophia about Justice attending a Broadway play at the Ethel Barrymore Theatre here in New York. She had warned Sophia to focus on men closer to her own age, but she'd been determined to meet Justice. That was the last day they'd spoken almost two weeks ago. Since then, she'd only received one text from Sophia saying that she was okay and was following her heart. All of their HCS ladies knew they had to check in daily if they were going away with a man, so she was worried and pissed that Sophia was jeopardizing the company and going rogue.

"What am I missing?" she wondered aloud before going on her computer to look at the personal file they had on Justice Covington again. There was a reason Sophia was interested in Justice, and why Savannah hadn't been able to track Justice's whereabouts lately in regards to his relationship status. Something wasn't adding up.

"Sir, you can't go in there," she heard Nina yell right before a man walked into her office, literally taking her breath away. *Tristan Derrington ... in the flesh.* God, he was sexy. Although she wished she could relish in his presence, the fact that he was standing in her office meant that HCS was in more trouble than she knew.

ABOUT THE AUTHOR

Sherelle Green is a Chicago native with a dynamic imagination and a passion for reading and writing. Ever since she was a little girl, Sherelle has enjoyed story-telling. Upon receiving her BA in English, she decided to test her skills by composing a fifty-page romance. The short, but sweet, story only teased her creative mind, but it gave her the motivation she needed to follow her dream of becoming a published author.

Sherelle loves connecting with readers and other literary enthusiasts, and she is a member of RWA and NINC. She's also an Emma award winner and two-time RT Book Reviews nominee. Sherelle enjoys composing novels that are emotionally driven and convey real relationships and real-life issues that touch on subjects that may pull at your heartstrings. Nothing satisfies her more than writing stories filled with compelling love affairs, multifaceted characters, and intriguing relationships.

For more information:

www.sherellegreen.com
authorsherellegreen.com

ALSO BY SHERELLE GREEN

An Elite Event Series:

A Tempting Proposal

If Only for Tonight

Red Velvet Kisses

Beautiful Surrender

Bare Sophistication Series:

Enticing Winter

Falling for Autumn

Waiting for Summer

Nights of Fantasy

Her Unexpected Valentine

Additional Books:

A Miami Affair

Wrapped in Red

Made in the USA
Middletown, DE
21 April 2018